Unwrapping Hope

Unwrapping Hope

A Widow's Might Novella

Sandra Ardoin

Corner Room Books

1

Library of Congress Control Number: 2019912825

ISBN: 978-1733463003 (print) | 978-1733463010 (ebook)

Cover design by Evelyne Labelle, Carpe Librum Book Design

Widow's Might Series
Unwrapping Hope
Enduring Dreams ~ Coming in 2020
Standalone Historicals
A Love Most Worthy
A Reluctant Melody
The Yuletide Angel

SANDRA ARDOIN

I sought the Lord, and he heard me,
and delivered me from all my fears.
Psalm 34:4

Chapter One

Phoebe Crain tightened her hold on her daughter's hand in case she got the notion to bolt down the street toward the Riverport train station.

"Mama, you said we'd go see the trains." Maura tugged on Phoebe, her stiff little body angled sideways, fully expecting her mother to comply. "Maybe he's there. Maybe he wants to be with us for Christmas."

The chug of an approaching engine and shrillness of the steam whistle mocked Phoebe with singsong lyrics: *Liar, liar. Liar, liar. Woo-woo!*

From Phoebe's other side, her mother whispered, "You should never have told her that story."

Meant only to appease, to avoid answering her five-year-old's questions, Phoebe had regretted her careless reply as soon as the words left her mouth.

Maura tugged again. "Come on, or we'll miss him."

Phoebe dreaded seeing disappointment again on Maura's face when they arrived at the station and the one she expected to meet was not there...whoever he was.

Liar, liar.

Lies destroyed relationships. Phoebe knew it too well, yet that hadn't prevented her from lying to her daughter. One day soon she must tell her little girl the truth. She would never find a papa waiting to meet her at the railroad station.

"Grandma has business at Newland's first."

Maybe by the time they had finished perusing the new five-and-ten-cent department—the only department where they could afford to shop—Maura would have forgotten about the train.

Doubtful.

A brisk walk led them to S. F. Newland's and Company, a commanding cousin of the general mercantile. Mud craters filled with rainwater huddled in the faint shadow cast across the street by the imposing four-story red brick building.

The door opened, and the young Mr. Newland stepped onto the sidewalk. Generally referred to as Spence, some people called him The Third and his father, The Second, nicknames neither Newland seemed to consider offensive.

Today he'd dressed in a gray wool overcoat with an expensive silk scarf wrapped around his neck. Judging by the trousers, he wore a fine wool suit under the coat.

He acknowledged them with an expedient nod. "Mrs. White. Mrs. Crain."

Phoebe pulled her coat collar closer to her neck to alleviate a sudden chill.

Mr. Newland grabbed the shiny black bicycle propped against the wall, mounted, then peddled down the muddy street without giving them a second glance. Not that Phoebe would have welcomed anything more from him. She had learned the hard way of the danger in even smiling at a young man with the means and superiority to entice what he wanted from a starry-eyed woman.

He peddled like his life depended on it. Perhaps he thought it did. Phoebe had heard he was obsessed with good health, maintaining his constitution with a proper diet and exercise.

"Look, Mama. It's a dollhouse." Maura yanked free and ran to the nearest front window. She pressed her mitten-covered hands against the glass and her forehead to the pane. "It's like Sarah's. Isn't it pretty?"

Awe mingled with longing in Maura's voice—a longing that made Phoebe want to weep because she could do nothing about it. Over and over her daughter talked of her friend's new toy and begged for one of her own.

The dollhouse in the window was as far beyond Phoebe's reach as the grand piano she had begged for in vain at fourteen. That, too, had been well beyond her mother's reach.

She crouched next to her little girl. Although the paint had been carelessly applied in spots and the wallpaper in the dining room was crooked, the dollhouse's homey appearance surpassed that of their own rented house. "It is lovely."

"See the tiny table and chairs?"

"Don't you think you would find it hard to sit in those chairs?"

Maura giggled. "They're not for me."

"They're not?" Phoebe grinned, then stood. "Grandma has gone inside. We'd better go in too."

After a long last stare through the window, Maura followed Phoebe into the store where the spices of the season greeted them—cinnamon, nutmeg, and cloves. The entrance to the large brick building smelled like a giant apple pie. Surely the scents alone had prompted a boon in the sale of kitchen products during the fall months.

Phoebe ignored most of the merchandise on well-placed counters, in glass cases, and on white-painted shelves. She tried to, anyway. Polite in her replies, she didn't stop when enticed by starched and smiling clerks who wanted to show her perfumes and hair combs or ribbons and dress collars trimmed with French lace. Why torment herself by lusting after frivolous things?

As she drew near a circular counter in the center of the store, a familiar voice called out, "Excuse me, Mrs. Crain."

She turned and smiled at the young man standing in the center. "Hello, Wallace."

Maura tugged on her hand. "I see Grandma. Can I go to her?"

Phoebe glanced down. "You can and you may." Once Maura had hold of her grandmother's coat, Phoebe stepped to the counter and asked Wallace, "Is your sister working today?"

"Yes, ma'am. Claire's at her station upstairs."

"Good. I'll go up in a bit to say hello."

Phoebe had met many wonderful women through her Widow's Might group, and Claire Kingsley had become one of Phoebe's closest friends in Riverport.

He motioned her closer. The ever-present smile on the young man's face held the power to light all four floors of the building. "I have something for you."

"Don't waste your time trying to sell me anything, Wallace."

"No, ma'am. I've been instructed to give you something." He reached under the counter, then handed her a square white box with a *S. F. Newland's and Company* label. The top was wrapped by a broad red velvet ribbon.

"A gift?" Why would someone leave her a gift, especially here? Why not deliver it to her personally? "Who is it from?"

His brow crinkled. "You don't know?"

"No."

"Then I can't say."

"Why not?"

"It's not my place, though I'm sure the gentleman who left it will make himself known to you soon."

A gentleman? She scanned the area around her. Was he watching, seeking her reaction? Of the few men present, none showed an interest in her.

Phoebe slipped off the ribbon, opened the lid of the outer box, and laid aside the thin paper on top. Her lips parted and her heartbeat accelerated. "I'm sure this is a mistake." She gently lifted the gift surrounded by a protective nest of tissue paper and marveled at the item crafted of burled maple and an intricate cherrywood inlay. When she raised the lid, the smell of tobacco hit her from the inclusion of a dozen cigars. Maura's father had owned a cigar box, but this one was much finer...and an outlandish gift for a woman.

Wallace released a soft whistle and grinned as he teased, "You smoke cigars, Mrs. Crain?"

A hint of a smile laced her quip. "Only every other Friday."

He peered inside the box. "Looks expensive."

"Yes." Too expensive to come without a price. This was a mistake by Wallace, and if it wasn't his mistake, keeping it would be hers. She slid it across the counter. "Here. Take it back."

"But it's a gift, and the gentleman will be disappointed."

"Better he's disappointed now than embarrassed later."

Wallace winked. "Might be from old St. Nick himself."

"It's far too early for St. Nick. Besides, he should know I grew up years ago. Even if I wanted to use this to store things other than cigars, I have nothing worthy of being housed in such a lovely case." Not anymore. "It's a mistake, so give it back to the person who left it here."

Wallace repacked it inside the outer box and slid it toward her. "I was told to give it to you. Please, Mrs. Crain, would you have me risk my job?"

Phoebe stared at the box. She wasn't eager to be the source of trouble for Claire's brother, so she picked it up from the counter. As she walked away to find her mother and Maura, Phoebe's gaze drifted toward the front window and the dollhouse.

Come Christmas Day, would she have anything pleasing to give her daughter? Would she ever?

Chapter Two

The first item on Spence's itinerary this afternoon was to confirm the delivery of his gift.

Standing inside S. F. Newland's and Company, he eyed the groups of women gathered around tantalizing displays. Though the store's inventory didn't ignore men, almost every department was designed to attract the attention of female shoppers.

His gaze skimmed the expansive first floor, highlighted by a wide staircase with wrought iron handrails. It led to two upper floors of merchandise with each floor fenced in by additional wrought iron. The elevator next to the stairs had been installed for the convenience of their less robust customers and those who worked on the fourth floor.

Every square foot of Newland's provided almost anything a customer could want, tempted her with much more than she needed, and did it all within a modern atmosphere of glass, marble, and electric lighting.

His father, Spencer Newland the Second, was an ingenious entrepreneur like Grandfather, Spencer the First. Nevertheless, the toll the '93 Panic had taken on their business and personal assets had almost closed this magnificent building.

After three hard years God had blessed their efforts and their numbers were growing again. Even so, Spence foresaw his idea of diversifying into five-and ten-cent stores as being critical to their future.

He glanced at the dollhouse in the window and shook his head.

Most of the time his father was ingenious. The machine-made work was shoddy and the materials cheap. However, according to Father, what mattered was bringing in parents who wanted to please their children. With Christmas a month away, they hoped to ensure that those customers entered and remained inside the store until they had completed buying their gifts.

His gaze narrowed on a couple near the perfumes. Gilbert Malone, their chief accountant and a college friend, gripped the arm of his wife, Roslyn—also a Newland's employee—in a firm hold and leaned in while he spoke to her. The anxiety on her face pointed to an unpleasant conversation. Normally they didn't employ married women, but he had done an old friend a favor. Now he hoped he hadn't made a mistake.

Before Spence could react, Gil let Roslyn go and stalked toward the elevator. She returned to her place behind the counter, hostility written in the glower she aimed at her husband's back.

The couple's behavior was unacceptable in the store, and he would have a word with the Malones later.

He crossed to the counter in the center of the first floor, where Wallace Pittman, one of the few male employees working outside the stockroom and offices, had finished providing a gentleman with the location of men's hats.

Spence glanced from side to side to be sure they weren't overheard by customers, then he asked Wallace, "Well?"

"She came in like you said, Mr. Newland."

"Good." When he discovered that potential investor Clifton Lark had a penchant for cigars, Spence had prepared a special gift for the businessman. However, Mr. Lark had sent his wife to Riverport for their meeting, a disappointing move but not bewildering given the rumors of his elusiveness during the past year.

"And you gave her the box?"

"Yes, sir."

"Nice work, Wallace."

Spence had expected Juliet Lark to come in for one last tour of their new five-and ten-cent section. Unable to see her off on her return to Chicago, he had instructed Wallace to give the box to the pretty brunette when she came in today.

"Funny thing, sir. She didn't want it and kept muttering, 'Must be a mistake.'"

Spence's grin died. He had asked Mrs. Lark to take the gift to her husband. Why would she think it a mistake?

With Juliet Lark's help, Spence had hoped to prove the Newlands's earnestness to do business with her husband. Securing the man's financial backing would assure his family that Spence's potential to lead their business interests was as great as that of his predecessors.

Maybe she hadn't liked the box. Maybe she considered it inferior work. What if her husband felt the same? What if Spence had tarnished the company's name?

"She was disappointed?"

"No, sir. Despite the surprise, I'd say she was tickled with it. In fact, I've never seen Mrs. Crain look so impressed."

Spence fought to breathe, his chest as tight as a debutante's corset. "D-Did you say Mrs. Crain?"

Wallace leaned over the counter and whispered, "Don't worry, Mr. Newland. I'll keep your lady friend's identity a secret."

Spence recoiled. "Mrs. Crain is not my lady friend."

She wasn't a friend at all. What he'd ever done to the woman was a mystery. She treated others with respect and friendliness, but from their first meeting, she had expressed her dislike of him through a constant cold shoulder.

"Why would you give my gift to Phoebe Crain?"

The clerk's eyes rounded. "Y-You told me to."

Spence gritted his teeth, then said, "The name I gave you was Mrs. Lark, not Mrs. Crain."

Wallace's eyebrows shot skyward. "I'm sorry, sir. I was looking at that new wallpaper right after you told me and guess I got confused. I mean, both women have bird names, and the wallpaper does have cranes on it."

Bird names? Cranes? Spence had seen that wallpaper. They were egrets. But that was beside the point.

"I should add that Mrs. Crain is a pretty brunette."

Spence pressed his balled fists against his thighs. Why hadn't he delegated the emergency with the lamp supplier to someone else and escorted Mrs. Lark onto the train? He could have given her the gift then.

He relaxed his hands. Although he'd had a brief introduction to Mrs. Lark the other day, Wallace wouldn't have connected the woman's importance to their future. This wasn't his fault. Much.

In addition, Mrs. Crain was a pretty brunette with a bird name.

Spence would get that box back and ship it to Chicago. Pronto. "It's fine, Wallace. It will be fine."

It must be fine. His reputation in the Newland family depended on it.

"IS THAT ANOTHER SCARF for a child at the orphanage?"

Phoebe glanced up from crocheting to answer her mother. "Yes, ma'am. I want to finish it before the next Widow's Might meeting."

She had suggested the group make scarves and mittens for the boys and girls as their charitable undertaking for the season. A few of their members had plentiful resources and provided most of the supplies. The rest, like Phoebe, were able to donate little more than their time and talents.

"You and your friends do good work for the children, Phoebe."

It was the least she could do to ease another's life. Like the apostle Paul, she had known what it was like to have much and what it was like to be in need.

Not all who resided at the Bethel Children's Home had lost a mother and father to death. For some, one parent lived. For others, one or both parents lived but couldn't afford to raise their children. They abandoned them to orphanages.

Lord, please don't ever place me in such a position with Maura. Not my baby.

In recent years Phoebe had wondered if her prayers fell on the ears of a deaf God. As much as she wanted to believe He heard her, nothing changed in her life.

Tired of dwelling on gloom, she said, "You should join us when we get together, Mama."

"I'm content with watching Maura and don't want to interfere in Verbenia's ministry."

"I'm sure she wouldn't think of it as interference. We're all friends."

Her mother set her Bible next to her on the sofa. "I could use some tea. How about you?"

The signal to end their conversation. "No, thank you."

The arthritis in Mama's hands had grown steadily worse. The pain and embarrassment over her gnarled fingers kept her from socializing and prevented steady employment. But Phoebe longed for her mother to find good friends in Riverport.

At a loud rap on the front door, Phoebe poked the crochet hook into the ball of wool yarn, set it aside, and opened the door.

What was he doing here?

"Good afternoon, Mrs. Crain." Spencer Newland the Third's smile broadened the slim face behind the hazelnut-colored mustache. At the same time, uncertainty flashed in his chestnut eyes. He shuffled his feet and rubbed his gloved hands together. "May I come in?"

"Why?" The word burst from her, followed by regret over the rude response.

His movements froze like the drips of icicles after sunset. "Because it's cold?"

By now almost anyone else would have been invited into the warmth of her home, but it wasn't that cold. He probably worried about an illness.

"I understand you have some unknown grievance against me, ma'am. This won't take long, and I'll be on my way."

With her mother here to act as a guardian, she tipped her head to gesture him inside.

"I'm afraid you received something of mine by mistake, Mrs. Crain. A small box wrapped with a red ribbon."

It belonged to *him*? The sooner she got rid of it and sent him on his way, the better.

"Just a moment." Phoebe entered the sitting room and opened the drawer in her mother's sewing cabinet, pulled out the white box, and carried it to him. "This?"

His shoulders relaxed. "Yes."

"It's stunning." She might resent men like him, but she could acknowledge beauty when she saw it.

His sparkling smile sent a shiver through her. "Thank you. It turned out to be one of my best pieces."

"You made this?"

"I did."

She opened the outer box and ran a finger over the wooden one inside—smooth as velvet and pieced together with the precision of an artisan. This wealthy and spoiled man had a talent she hadn't expected of him.

An idea percolated in Phoebe's mind and refused the inner warning that said it was wrong. It might be her only chance to give her little girl the Christmas she deserved.

He reached for the box, but she whisked it from his grasp. "I have a request, Mr. Newland."

"A request?"

Phoebe vacillated. She had no right to withhold the box and almost handed it over, until she remembered Maura's awe as she'd gazed through the store's window that afternoon.

"What can I do for you, Mrs. Crain?"

Still smiling, his voice was tinged with the calm of an experienced salesman, as though he would grant her every wish. She had seen that look before. This time she denied its persuasive power. "My daughter has her heart set on a dollhouse. I can't afford the one in your store window but would like her to receive a similar one for Christmas."

With a slight tilt of his head, he watched her through wary pupils.

Simply ask him in a polite and friendly manner to build Maura a dollhouse.

How could she? She had no money to pay for it and refused to be indebted to him. One day he would decide to take advantage of that debt. Wasn't that the way men like him operated?

"I'm suggesting an exchange."

Both the calm and the smile disappeared from his face. "Let me be sure I understand. You would keep what you received in error and hold it for ransom in exchange for a shabbily made dollhouse?"

"I said similar to the one in the window, Mr. Newland. I'm not asking for that one. Judging by what I'm holding, I'm convinced you can build something much nicer."

His lips parted as if he wasn't sure how to respond to her compliment.

"I'm merely proposing a trade. But if you prefer not to deal..." She placed the lid on the container.

His laugh was hoarse and humorless. "I knew you were as frosty as a windowpane. I had no idea your flaws sank to the depths of extortion."

Her jaw tensed at the same time her fingers tightened on the box. *And I knew you were no better than other young men in your social circle.*

With as much dignity as Phoebe could muster under the circumstances, she walked around him to the door and opened it. "Good day, Mr. Newland."

He hesitated. Despite the cold seeping into her house, beads of perspiration clung to her upper lip.

His attention shifted to take in the entire front room. Perhaps she imagined the slight wrinkling of his nose but didn't think so. Evidently, the poor rich man had never seen a house with such sparse furnishings and worn wallpaper. His attention focused on the piano at the far wall. "You are not sorry for keeping my box?"

Phoebe wavered, then said, "No, sir."

He stomped outside without saying another word. Once he'd reached his fancy new safety bicycle at the edge of the street, she shut the door and pressed her back against the wood. He might not realize she'd just told a lie, but God knew.

She closed her eyes. Mr. Newland was right. She had sunk to the level of an extortionist.

"What have you done, Phoebe?"

Her eyes popped open to see her mother standing at the other end of the hallway.

"What were you thinking? His family is influential in this town, and you're just—"

"I know. I'm nothing. I've heard it before."

After a heavy sigh, her mother walked toward her. "You know I didn't mean that."

Phoebe stepped away from the door and held out the box. "Look at this. I've never seen such handiwork. If he can create something this lovely and intricate, a dollhouse for Maura would be a simple project for him."

Mama stopped a foot away, her attention locked on Phoebe, not the box. "It doesn't make what you've done right."

"No, but for the first time in her life, Maura would receive something special for Christmas, something I can't give her." When her mother continued to stare at her, Phoebe defended her decision. "It won't cost him anything but time and a few materials that he can easily afford."

Mama wrapped her arms around her and drew her close, sharing the warmth of body and spirit. "Perhaps, my dear Phoebe. But what will it cost you?"

If she continued to feel no cleaner than the dirt under Mr. Newland's feet, it would cost her too much. How was her treatment of The Third any more noble than the way Douglas had treated her? The circumstances between Phoebe and Maura's father were different, but the result was the same—manipulation and abuse.

Phoebe pulled away. "You're right, Mama. It was a momentary lapse."

Hoping to catch Mr. Newland before he got away, she carried the box outside and hurried down the walk. Anger probably propelled his bicycle at top speed, because she searched each end of the street to no avail.

After returning to the house, she told her mother, "I'll take it to him when I finish my lessons tomorrow."

At the same time, she would eat the crow she already smelled cooking.

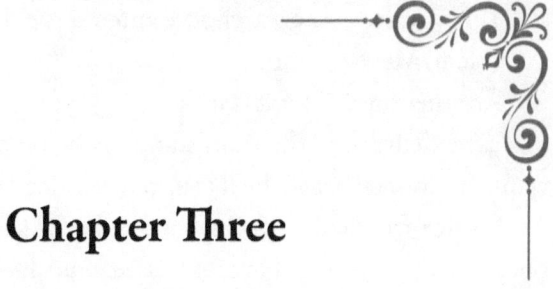

Chapter Three

S pence glanced at the clock on his office wall. Fifteen hours since he had become a victim of Mrs. Crain's attempt at extortion.

Phoebe Crain's attitude toward him left him dazed, off kilter. They were close in age, but in her presence he often felt like a ten-year-old facing disapproval by an older and wiser adult without ever knowing what he'd done wrong. In some ways she reminded him of his grandfather.

His hands tightened around the arms of his office chair. No matter how much he might want to help the child, he refused to be manipulated into building her a dollhouse even if her mother had flattered him with her remarks about the quality of the cigar box. On the other hand, making another box would take precious time. What else could he do to attract the man's interest?

Adding to his troubles this morning, their warehouse manager had notified him of more missing inventory. Newland's dealt with its share of shoplifters, but these losses involved merchandise they had paid for and either hadn't received or had come up missing before reaching the floor. How could it be?

Spence faced his desk and shuffled invoices and correspondence around like they were cards in a euchre game. Outside his office, people carried on with their work while he stewed and achieved little progress.

"Mr. Newland?"

Spence's hand jerked and left a trail of ink across the paper in front of him. He scowled at the involuntary mark. "Come in, Amos."

The man from the warehouse entered the room. "I'm afraid there's a problem, Mr. Newland."

Another one? "What is it?"

"The delivery at the train station is being held up. Eugene Henry wants his money before he'll transport the load to the store."

Spence frowned. "Mr. Henry has been delivering for us since we opened five years ago. He knows that's not how we operate. Did you remind him he's to invoice us and wait until the accountant pays his bill?"

"Yes, sir, but he says he wants payment now. Maybe you can talk some sense into him."

Talk sense into the man? He couldn't even convince a woman to return something that wasn't hers. Maybe his grandfather had been right about him. He wasn't strong—physically or intellectually.

No, he'd fought too hard to prove the man wrong. "I'll handle it, Amos."

Spence considered riding his bicycle, but he hadn't had time for his calisthenics this morning. He could use a brisk walk. It would give him time to clear his head of yesterday's blunder and make room for ideas about how to convince Eugene Henry to do his job.

The deliveryman stood in the railroad yard, his face angled down and partially hidden by a black cap. Behind him were stacked nearly a dozen large crates. He paced back and forth with his hands stuffed in the pockets of a plaid wool coat. His teen son sat on the bench of a freight wagon, ready to help his father load and unload Newland's new merchandise—if they could come to an agreement.

Spence approached the delivery man and held out his hand. "Mr. Henry, it's good to see you again."

Eugene returned the handshake. "I'm guessing you're not here to see to my health, Mr. Newland."

A tightness surrounded Eugene's mouth, and worry lines creased his forehead. Dark circles underlined his eyes. Spence took an involuntary step backward and caught himself before going farther. "Are you ill?"

Eugene backed against the crates, and his shoulders sagged. "Not me. My wife."

"I'm sorry." Anyone who knew Spence would realize the truth in his statement. "I understand we have a problem. What can I do to solve it?"

With a slight turn of his head, Eugene stared off down the tracks. "Sir, you can pay me today for this delivery."

"We pay our bills promptly. There's no need to anticipate a delay."

"I need the money now." He shrugged. "Truth is, I can't afford to buy the medicine Doc says my wife needs in order to get better."

Even though Spence understood his plight, understanding didn't get the crates delivered to the store. He could pay Eugene as requested, but if word got around, other hired creditors might demand payment in advance, which would create more problems for the store.

Eugene was not the only man in town capable of making deliveries, and plenty of men were desperate for work. On the other hand, if word got out that the owners of Newland's hired someone else and refused to help the Henry family, they would appear callous and without compassion.

Even more crucial, Mrs. Henry's health depended on receiving the medicine.

After all Spence had undergone in his younger years, how could he withhold essential treatment from someone else?

He peered round the rail yard. On the other side of the tracks, the Wabash River, so busy with traffic and trade in his grandfather's day, flowed with minor interruption, its necessity for transporting goods replaced by the railroads. Times had changed, but people's troubles had not.

He lowered his voice. "How much do you need?"

"A dollar would get me by."

It wasn't like the man was demanding the moon—or a dollhouse—and he'd proved himself trustworthy in the past.

Spence dug in his pocket and handed him the money. "Here. Let's keep this between you and me."

Eugene paused, then took the coins. The lines between his eyes smoothed. "Thank you, sir. I won't say a thing to nobody."

"See that your wife receives the medicine before making your delivery."

The Henrys left, and Spence strolled closer to the tracks. His cold nose couldn't compete with the warmth he felt inside over seeing Eugene's relief.

"You're a nice man, mister."

Spence twisted sideways and peeked around the stacks of merchandise. A girl of five or six sat on the track side of the crates. Her smile, missing a front tooth, brightened the dreary day. "I did the right thing?"

"You made him happy."

"Well, let's keep it our secret, shall we?"

She placed a finger to her closed mouth, and he laughed.

The girl looked familiar. "What's your name?"

"Maura, sir."

"Why are you sitting here alone, Miss Maura?"

"I'm waiting."

"Waiting for what?"

"That train."

She pointed down the track. An engine chugged toward the station, gray steam billowing from the chimney. A number of passenger and freight cars trailed behind.

"Is there something special about that train?"

"It might have my papa on it."

Spence noted a handful of people gathered for the train's arrival. A young woman stood near the wall of the station building. She watched him with the eyes of a human hawk. He tilted his head in her direction and said to Maura, "You should join your mother."

"She's not my mama."

The train screeched to a halt. It huffed and puffed as it disgorged porters and a few passengers. Maura's gaze fixed on each person who arrived.

The woman near the two-story building lost interest in Spence and Maura, strolled to the first car, and disappeared inside. Once everyone had boarded, the engine belched and pulled away from the Riverport station, leaving him alone with the little girl, whose mouth formed a petite pout. Why hadn't her father arrived as she'd expected?

"Where is your mother?" Spence asked.

"Playing the piano."

What kind of mother put playing the piano ahead of her daughter's safety and welcoming her husband home?

"She sent you to meet your father?"

Maura hung her head. "Her and Grandma don't know I left."

Grandma? It was as though every electric light bulb in Newland's chandeliers illuminated the answer, and he realized where he had seen Maura before. Yesterday, after he'd left Mrs. Lark's gift with Wallace and walked out of the store, he'd noticed the girl with her mother. She'd stared longingly at the dollhouse he'd called shoddy and acted as if she had never seen anything so beautiful. By the look of the place he had visited last evening, perhaps she hadn't.

"You're Mrs. Crain's daughter."

Her little head bobbed.

Spence had understood Mrs. Crain was a widow. However, according to Maura, her father wasn't dead but soon to join his family. "You say your mother is playing the piano?"

"Teddy's there for his lesson."

Her crinkled nose reminded him of his reaction to the forlorn sitting room he'd seen. It was an ill-mannered reaction, but no ruder than her mother holding hostage his gift to Clifton Lark.

"Teddy plays like a wailing cat with his tail stuck in the door."

Spence turned his laugh into a cough.

Surely Mrs. Crain had noted her daughter's disappearance by now and must be worried. He pulled out his pocket watch and checked the time. A mound of paperwork remained on his desk to be completed before a meeting with The Second this afternoon. He'd wasted enough time but couldn't shoo Maura home without an escort and not worry about her the rest of the day. And she was too young for him to leave here by herself.

He glanced around. What if he hired someone to drive her?

He'd still worry.

Spence peered at the little girl, who gazed at him with bright brown eyes and a sunshine smile minus a tooth. He held out a hand. "Come along, Miss Maura. I'll take you home."

She gave the tracks one last look up and down. With a high-pitched sigh, she reached for his hand. The fragility in her small grip sparked a fierce protectiveness in him.

Her coat sleeve was rolled to her wrist. The other sleeve draped her hand. The worn coat hung on her, a stark contrast to the cut and quality of his clothes and a reminder of Mrs. Crain's request. He enjoyed helping others when possible. Why hadn't she just asked him to build the girl a dollhouse? Why had she employed a more devious means?

Hadn't Eugene Henry done much the same? He'd held Newland's merchandise hostage for a dollar's worth of medicine. So why give in to the delivery man and not Mrs. Crain when there wasn't much difference in their actions?

There was a difference—possibly, a life and death difference. Medicine meant much more than a toy, no matter how endearing the recipient.

Spence recalled the relief on the man's face. He had done a good deed.

UNWRAPPING HOPE

Maura Crain said so.

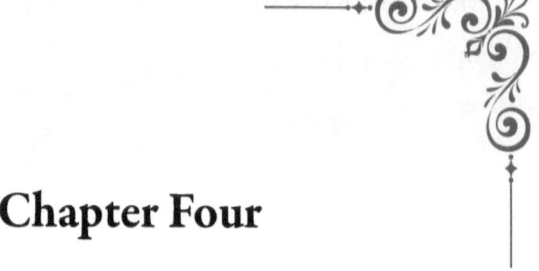

Chapter Four

"**N**o, Teddy, dear. *Legato*. Listen carefully." For the third time in the past ten minutes Phoebe repeated the chord for her pupil. "Play the notes in a smooth manner with no silence, no hesitation in between."

The upright piano, though somewhat battered and purchased secondhand, was an extravagant item, considering the rest of her possessions, but one she would never sell, as she had done with her jewelry and all but one of her evening dresses. Without the instrument, she had no livelihood.

Even so, if she wanted to continue to pay the rent, she must enroll more students. The tuition of those she taught now barely covered the monthly expenses. Hopefully, she would be blessed with a few more pupils who possessed a musical competence.

Phoebe winced at the sour piano note that pierced her ears. With gentleness and tact, she had told Mrs. Barrett to save her money on lessons because Teddy had no interest in playing the piano. She'd left off saying he had six thumbs. Perhaps she should have added that opinion, because the woman didn't believe her son possessed no talent or inclination to develop it.

While Teddy was a sweet boy, any more like him and she might switch to cleaning chimneys for a living...or resort to performing for the wealthy's social gatherings again.

No, those days ended six years ago. She would prefer cleaning chimneys to being in the same place with men who reminded her of

Maura's father.

The boy sneezed and wiped his nose on his sleeve.

"Phoebe"—her mother trotted into the sitting room—"have you seen Maura?"

With the urgency in her voice, Phoebe's insides bounced like Teddy's fingers on the keys. She jumped from the chair alongside the piano stool. "You sent her out back to play."

"I checked on her, and she wasn't there."

"Have you looked in the bedroom?"

"I've looked throughout the house."

"And out front?"

"Front and back. Down the street." Her mother's voice rose with panic as she twisted her knotted hands. "Where could she have gone?"

"We'll find her." Phoebe would find her. "Mrs. Barrett should be here shortly. Why don't you stay with Teddy while I look for Maura."

She slipped into her coat and fumbled with the buttons. Her scrabbling fingers exposed her anxiety. She flung open the front door and almost ran into the person on the other side. Him again?

"I'm afraid I don't have time to talk to you, Mr. Newland."

"Nor I you, Mrs. Crain."

When a small face peeked from behind him, Phoebe's heart thudded with relief. "Maura." She crouched and reached her arms out. Her child fell into them. "We were worried."

"I'm sorry, Mama. This man found me." Maura peered up at her companion as if the palm of his hand held the moon.

Years ago Phoebe had seen a similar look in the mirror. If she could go back in time, she would shatter the glass.

She rose and pressed her daughter to her side. "I'm grateful, Mr. Newland. Where was she?"

He smiled down at Maura. "At the train station."

She should have guessed. "Maura, I've told you to never go there by yourself."

The child hung her head. "He didn't come, Mama."

"I'm sorry, sweetheart." Phoebe spoke around a lump the size of a caboose.

Her mother said, "I'll take Maura and Teddy to the kitchen."

"But I want to stay with Mr. Newland. He's nice. He gave a man a dollar so he could buy medicine for his sick wife." Maura slapped her hand over her mouth and mumbled something about a secret.

The hint of a flush colored Mr. Newland's cheeks. He had done something kind and wanted to keep it secret? Why?

"Go with Grandma."

"Goodbye, Miss Maura."

The three of them left the room, and hushed moments passed between Phoebe and the man who had seen to Maura's safe return. She was grateful to him. Truly. Anything could have happened to her daughter while alone at the train station.

"Thank you for seeing Maura home." The simple statement seemed too insignificant, too matter of fact for the courtesy he had done her family. But why couldn't someone else have returned her? Why must he be the object of Phoebe's gratitude?

"She's a friendly child."

"Very."

This was her chance to make amends for last night. "If you'll wait a moment." She retrieved the box and returned to the door. Her grip on it tensed before she summoned the resolve to place it in his hands. "You were right. This belongs to you. I apologize for my behavior. It was wrong of me to...to use it as I did."

He took the box, and in his steady regard, he seemed to peer into her mind, looking for the answer to her change of heart. He'd find nothing but guilt and, perhaps, a hint of fear over the compulsion to answer his smile with one of her own.

"Thank you."

Now that he had met Maura and liked her, might he be more

willing to build her a dollhouse? "Mr. Newland..."

The question froze on Phoebe's tongue. What was she doing? She'd had a momentary bout of insanity last night. No use in repeating it and being shamed again. Besides, if he did agree, it meant more contact with him. Given her history, that was akin to placing herself in the path of a rampaging bull.

"Yes?"

Rather than a dollhouse, Maura would receive socks for Christmas again this year. "Never mind."

"Then I'll leave you to continue your lesson. Good day." He twisted away, faltered, then turned back again. "It's none of my business, but Maura told me she was waiting for her father at the railroad station."

If only Phoebe could find a hole to crawl into. "I'm aware of Maura's purpose for being there, but she knows her father died before she was born."

"I see."

No, he didn't see, but thankfully, didn't ask for details.

Once Teddy left, she would sit Maura down and explain that men didn't arrive on trains with the aim of becoming fathers.

Somehow, she would find a way to buy Maura the dollhouse in the window of Newland's.

WALLACE LET PHOEBE inside the Pittman home, his face as red as a ripe tomato. "Before you say anything, Mrs. Crain, I apologize for what happened at the store the other day. It was my fault for confusing you and Mrs. Lark."

Mrs. Lark? The Third had meant the cigar box for a woman after all? Strange.

"Don't worry, Wallace. It's over."

His bearing relaxed, and he led her down the hall to the comfortable sitting room made even more cozy when all eight ladies attended the Widow's Might meetings. "Mrs. Jensen is the only other one to arrive."

Months ago, Verbenia Jensen had invited her to join the group of Riverport widows who referred to themselves as Widow's Might. As their elder mentor, Verbenia was the durable thread that kept the emotions of each member of the circle from unraveling.

Phoebe enjoyed her time with the ladies and the worthwhile projects they undertook, but she dreaded the day when they realized she was a fraud.

"Go on in, Mrs. Crain," Wallace said. "I'll help Claire with the refreshments."

Phoebe sneezed.

"The Lord bless you."

Phoebe dabbed a handkerchief against her nose. With a nasal voice, she said, "I don't know what's come over me. This is the third time I've sneezed today."

"I hope you're not coming down with anything."

"It's probably something in the air." Or a result of Teddy Barrett's runny nose.

Verbenia patted the sofa seat, urging Phoebe to join her. "How is everything?"

The question carried more weight than the type of casual comment most people threw out simply to fill a silent moment. The woman tended to draw honesty and confession even from Phoebe. "Christmas will be here soon, and I'm not sure I'll have a gift for Maura, not what she wants."

"And what is that?"

"A dollhouse." And a father. "She'll get socks again."

"There's nothing wrong with a gift of practicality."

Phoebe breathed a soft snort. "Maura has never received a gift that wasn't practical. She's too little to understand financial matters, so I dread disappointing her another year."

"It doesn't take extravagance to make a child happy, dear. She might mope for a while, but she knows how much you love her and will get over any disappointment." Verbenia clasped Phoebe's forearm and gave it a little squeeze. "Perhaps there's another way to provide what she wants."

"Another way?"

"My daughter tells me there's a store in Cincinnati that has hired a quartet to provide music for customers during the holiday season. You could suggest it to one of the Newlands."

Phoebe had suggested enough to Spence Newland lately. She doubted he would be receptive to any additional ideas she put forward.

She inhaled the mild and pleasant citrus scent of the verbena toilet water her friend adored. "You're an employee of the store. That sounds like something that should come from you."

"I don't play the piano, and you do."

The door buzzer sounded, and Verbenia stood. "That must be the others."

Laughter and the clatter of multiple pairs of shoes sounded in the hall. A moment later Claire led the rest of the ladies into the sitting room. The tall and reserved Edythe Westin brought up the rear. As usual, the widow and mother of three was dressed in the height of fashion. Despite her wealth, Edythe was one of the sweetest people Phoebe had ever met. It seemed her bias only focused on the males of Edythe's social status.

As she smiled and greeted her friends, Phoebe reconsidered Verbenia's idea. Her first thought had been a resounding no. She no longer played for an audience of strangers and told herself she had no desire to return to that life.

But didn't her daughter deserve a happy Christmas?

Chapter Five

When his housekeeper announced the visit by Mrs. Crain and Mrs. Jensen, Spence almost wrenched his neck to eye the entrance hall for a glimpse of the young widow.

"Show them to the drawing room, please, Mrs. Rosenbach. I'll be in shortly." He set aside the note he'd been writing to ship with the cigar box, unrolled his shirtsleeves, and shrugged into the suit coat draped across the back of the desk chair.

What did the ladies want with him at his home on this late Sunday afternoon? On any afternoon for that matter? Maybe Mrs. Crain thought she'd try once more to press him into making her daughter a dollhouse. Then again, with the presence of Mrs. Jensen, it might mean they were collecting for a charity.

Since the return of the cigar box, he'd found it hard to think of much more than the woman and her charming little girl. What had changed Phoebe Crain's mind? Gratitude?

He crossed the hall and found his guests poised on the edge of the drawing room's striped davenport. Mrs. Crain sat with her back straight and her profile set in stone. Frankly, even stony, it was a nice profile.

"Good afternoon, ladies."

Both women stood at his entrance. Mrs. Jensen smiled. "Good afternoon, Mr. Newland. What a lovely home."

"Thank you." Given Mrs. Crain's animosity toward him, there wasn't much point in chitchat. "What brings you two to see me?"

Mrs. Jensen gave her companion an encouraging nod, and Mrs.

Crain inhaled, as if she needed courage. She sneezed.

With his childhood propensity for taking ill, he affected a smile but kept his distance from her. He wouldn't put it past her to come here to share a cold with him.

"Excuse me." She pressed a handkerchief to her pink nose, then balled it in her hand. "Mr. Newland, are you aware that a Cincinnati store has hired a quartet to provide music during the holidays?" The words rushed out as though, if she didn't hurry, she would keep her purpose for coming bottled inside.

Spence didn't admit to being ignorant of her news. If she knew something like that, why didn't he? "Please have a seat."

She retook her spot on the davenport, and the flowers in her dress clashed with the material surrounding her. He settled in the armchair a few feet away and waited.

"I-I think you should consider such a thing for your store. Besides providing entertainment, I believe it will relax your customers and encourage them to spend more money." She voiced the latter part of her statement with a hint of humor, just enough to keep him from considering it impertinent. "Music often has the power to soothe people."

"You think it's a good business idea to hire someone to play for our customers?" He restrained his amusement over the sly attempt to steer him into offering her employment.

"I see the merit in it."

"What about you, Mrs. Jensen? As an employee, you know our customers. Do you believe their time in the store will be enhanced by background music?"

A twinkle lit the woman's blue eyes. "I do, sir."

Now he understood why Verbenia Jensen sat in his drawing room. Not only was she a chaperone, she was Mrs. Crain's champion.

He turned to Phoebe. "You play the piano, Mrs. Crain, so I assume you think Newland's would do well to hire you."

She raised her chin with confidence. "I do."

"Where did you learn to play?"

"My mother was housekeeper to a concert pianist who saw potential in me at an early age. He insisted I learn. He was an amazing man." She cleared her voice of its wistfulness and added, "My benefactor didn't want people to connect me with my mother, so I performed in music halls under the name Phoebe Langford."

The name was familiar.

"You're Phoebe Langford?" Verbenia Jensen's mouth opened with awe. "My son and his wife saw you perform in Chicago. They said you were magnificent. Oh, my dear, I never knew. Why didn't you tell us?"

Before the conversation got away from its intent, Spence said, "You must have started young."

Phoebe squeezed the handkerchief. "I began at sixteen and performed throughout the Midwest. While doing so, I learned the finer points of circulating in society—how to talk, walk, act, dress. I won't be an embarrassment to S. F. Newland's and Company."

Spence didn't doubt it, but he still frowned. With a background like that, why had she quit the concert stage? For marriage? "Do you miss performing before audiences?"

She shifted her attention to her hands. "No."

Which of them was she trying to convince?

He pointed to the grand piano near the window, amazed he was considering her suggestion. "I'd like to hear you play."

Mrs. Crain took a seat on the bench. "Is there anything in particular you would like to hear?"

"I'll leave it up to you."

The familiar piece began calm and unhurried. Soon Spence's vision worked to keep up with her fingers as they danced over the keys. Finally, he followed Mrs. Jensen's example and shut his eyes, letting his ears do the work. Phoebe Langford—or Crain, if she preferred—had chosen one of the hardest compositions known.

After the last note faded, he said, "'Étude No. 6.'"

"You know Listz?"

"I've attempted to play that piece on occasion. Unlike you, I failed."

She rose from the piano stool, her face flushed from the exertion. "You found it satisfactory?"

Highly. "Yes. It was satisfactory."

The optimism expressed in Mrs. Crain's shining and fervent gaze dimmed at his halfhearted response. Mrs. Jensen studied him. Her arched brow said she found his comment astonishing.

Why hadn't he said what he really thought? Phoebe Crain was a brilliant musician. Had he restrained his praise because her stiff upper lip unsettled him? Because it irritated him to think the change from her normally cool attitude stemmed from her desire for employment? He hoped he wasn't that petty but feared it was true.

She sneezed again and apologized.

Hire her.

He quenched the inner command and guided the ladies to the hall, making sure to stay away from Maura's mother. He had no time to be bedridden and had spent too many days over the years as an invalid to desire a return to that state. "Thank you for coming, Mrs. Crain. I'll let you know my decision."

Mrs. Jensen said goodbye and waited on the porch.

Mrs. Crain paused by the door. She opened her mouth and shut it again. Her head bobbed. "Good day, Mr. Newland."

Spence peered through the side panel next to the door as she walked down the sidewalk to the street. Her bearing was erect, as though signaling that his lack of enthusiasm would not affect her.

She conducted herself in a well-bred and well-educated fashion. Her gentle mannerisms and cultured speech reflected that of a lady accustomed to mixing in society. She possessed a talent he envied, yet she struggled to provide for her family. Why?

Spence often saw her as a snarling guard dog. On occasion, she reminded him of a vulnerable stray—one whose mistrust said she suspected him of a nefarious intent. For the life of him, he couldn't understand what he'd done to give her that idea.

Maybe that was why he hadn't obeyed the urge to hire her on the spot.

Phoebe Crain was a mystery that begged to be solved.

PHOEBE LIFTED THE COVERS on her bed. She might be better to try to lift the butcher's draft horse. With the attempt to sit up, her head swam, and she sank back into the mattress, issuing a low groan that was like slicing the inside of her throat with a knife.

Her mother opened the bedroom door and peeked into the room. "Phoebe, it's eight o'clock. Why are you still in bed?"

"B-Because..." Phoebe coughed and pressed her fingertips against each side of her throbbing head.

Mama crossed the room and felt her forehead. "You have a fever." She settled the covers around Phoebe's shoulders and neck.

Phoebe gazed at the empty bed on the other side of the room. "Maura..."

"The child is fine. I'll take care of her. You stay here and rest."

"I...can't." Phoebe cleared her throat, but her voice was little more than a hoarse whisper when she added, "I have...students."

"Do you think their mothers will want them sick too? What will that do for their wish to send their children to you?"

She had a point.

Mama felt her head again. "It's not bad, but I should send for a doctor."

"Can't...afford it." Speaking hurt her raw throat, but Phoebe couldn't let her mother waste money on a doctor's fee to tell her she had a cold. She couldn't afford to miss the income from her lessons either. Another groan skipped like a rock on the surface of the Wabash River.

Oh, that Teddy!

"I'll make you some hot tea and honey to soothe your throat," her mother said.

Phoebe nodded. The sooner she was well, the sooner she could get back to work.

"You should be up and around in a few days."

Days? "No, I..." She swallowed, wincing at the rawness. By the time she could speak again, her mother had left the room.

What if Mr. Newland decided he would hire her to play piano in the store? What if he wanted her to start today or tomorrow?

A croaky laugh bubbled up. What chance had she of being hired when his response to her playing was as exciting as a yawn?

He had humiliated her yesterday, and she had to admit it was well deserved. By the time she had left his house, she'd felt so small she could have walked out under his front door.

If necessary, she would face more embarrassment, because she would do anything for her child.

She shut her eyes and let her mind drift to the first time Douglas had heard her play. He'd brought her red roses and talked the stage manager into granting him access behind the theater curtain. He'd fawned over her talent, clapping and smiling and shouting "Bravo!" Maura's father had made her feel as though she owned the world that night.

From then on, Phoebe had fallen for every lie he'd told.

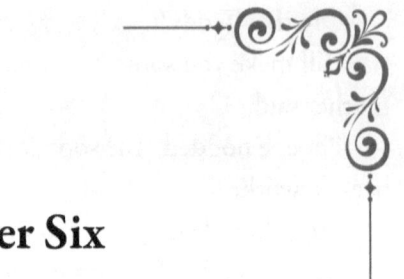

Chapter Six

S pence made the mistake of arriving at Phoebe's home near the end of another lesson with Teddy. With all the effort he could muster, he waited on the sofa and cringed at the notes the boy missed, the ones he played by mistake, and his poor sense of timing—even with the help of a metronome.

A wailing cat with its tail in the door.

Secure as a bank vault, his lips sealed in the amusement over Maura's accurate description of the boy's competence at the piano—or lack of it. This suffering was his own fault for not hiring Mrs. Crain on Sunday, then insisting he'd wait until the boy's lesson was over to speak with her today.

The furniture in the room was tasteful though worn and sparse. A pile of sheet music sat in an old crate atop a small table near the piano. The teacher could use a music cabinet.

"That's enough for today, Teddy." Phoebe covered his hands with hers, stopping the erratic crescendo. Evidently, even she couldn't bear it any more. "Your mother will be here soon."

The boy spun on the stool and hightailed it to the front hall for his coat, as if that cat's tail were on fire.

Maura called for her mother, and Mrs. Crain shot Spence an apologetic glance. "I should see what she wants. She's in bed and not well."

Spence made a mental note to send the child something to cheer her. "Tell Miss Maura I hope she feels better soon."

Phoebe Crain mumbled a thank-you in a voice deeper than normal and left the room.

He rose and walked into the hall. "Tell me something, Teddy. Don't you enjoy playing the piano?"

The boy's mouth twisted. "I stink at it. I'd rather play baseball."

Spence had never played sports. He'd been too sickly as a child. His activities consisted of reading, music, and building primitive wooden objects in his room, but he could understand the boy's desire to rebel against doing what he stank at.

As much as he enjoyed working at Newland's, if Spence couldn't convince Lark to help them expand into the growing five-and-ten-cent-store market, he'd stink at proving himself a productive member of the Newland family.

"I like Mrs. Crain," Teddy said. "She's nice. Ma says she and the rest of them Widow's Might women are a treasure."

"Widow's Might? What is that?"

Teddy shrugged. "I don't know. It's just somethin' I heard her say. You'd better ask Mrs. Crain." He bolted out the front door before anyone could order him to return to the piano.

Never.

When Mrs. Crain returned, she said, "I'm sorry you had to wait. Tomorrow is Thanksgiving, and I wanted to get in Teddy's lesson beforehand."

No doubt she needed the money from every student. She was far too young to be saddled with so much responsibility and solemnity.

Given the sickness in this house, Spence shouldn't have stayed, but he lowered his voice and said, "Has anyone told you that you sound like a too-bah today?" He slid one arm out straight and tucked it back, blowing a note through the hand curled against his mouth.

She raised her chin in a gesture that said she would not be amused. No, she would not. But her puckered lips betrayed her. She crossed her arms. "That is a trombone, Mr. Newland, not a tuba."

He pretended to study the invisible instrument in his hand. "So it is."

Despite a valiant attempt to hold it in, a croaky chuckle escaped from her.

His eyes widened in feigned surprise. "Now doesn't laughter make you feel better?" It had always made him feel better.

"There's nothing wrong with me." Her expression sobered, and her brown eyes—as soft as the velvet covering a deer's antlers—held a smidgeon of hope. "You've made up your mind?"

Father doubted the plan would pay for itself but left the decision to Spence. After days spent mulling over the plusses and minuses of employing Phoebe, he had decided to limit her presence to two days per week for the upcoming holidays. The time would allow him to test the idea of adding music to the customer experience and limit his exposure to this woman who awed him in both positive and negative ways.

"Newland's would be pleased to welcome your talent in our store. What hours would interfere least with your private lessons on Fridays and Saturdays?"

"I could do"—she cocked her head, her focus on the wall behind him before it switched back to him—"two hours in the afternoon. Two to four?"

"And two hours in the morning? Ten to twelve?"

"That's a lot of time out of my day."

She was determined to make everything involving him as hard as possible. "It's only for a month."

"Well, I suppose I could rearrange my schedule." She forced her shoulders back in a "there's more" stance. "I'll require a high-quality instrument."

"I'll have my personal piano delivered to the store this afternoon." The sparkle in her eyes told him she had hoped that was what he'd say. "You'll start Friday morning at ten."

"I'll be there." She stopped him at the front door. "One more thing, Mr. Newland."

Now what?

"I would prefer no one knows I'm Phoebe Langford."

First thing Monday morning, he had wired a friend whose responses to his questions convinced him she could very well be the pianist. Even so, he wasn't willing to risk the reputation of the store by claiming an uncertainty.

"I agree." He buttoned his coat and adjusted the scarf around his neck against the chill breeze outside. "I'll see you Friday?"

"Yes."

After a few more instructions, Spence turned his bicycle in the direction of the store and cast a last glance at Phoebe's frail little house, hearing once more her gravelly chuckle.

Seeing that smile, no matter how begrudgingly it came, had done something to him—something he was afraid to name.

"GRANDMA'S TAKING ME to see the trains. Maybe he'll be there today."

Phoebe pulled her daughter aside and out of the way of a customer entering the department store. Next time she would enter through the employee door at the rear of the building. "Maura, we've discussed this. What I told you before was only a fairy tale based on how I met your father. It won't happen that way a second time."

"But it could." Maura's voice rose to a shrill whine.

A gentleman bumped Phoebe's shoulder and apologized. With people coming and going, this was not the time or place to continue the conversation. Mr. Newland expected her to begin her job in fifteen minutes. "God will bring you a papa when He deems it's time."

Even if it made her daughter happy, Phoebe was in no hurry for that particular gift. Not that she scorned marriage. She believed happy unions were possible—with the right man.

"Don't forget to give Mr. Newland my drawing."

"I won't." Phoebe hugged the child, then stood and handed her off to her mother. "I'll be home for lunch."

She inhaled a crisp, bracing breath before walking farther into the store. Only her desire to provide Maura with something nice for Christmas persuaded her to accept this job, especially after Mr. Newland had tried to charm her with his teasing about the trombone...and it had worked.

After losing two days of pay through illness, and considering she'd lose more wages because of the holiday, every penny earned here would go toward making up the income before she could apply whatever remained to Maura's dollhouse. Hopefully, she'd be able to put a little aside too.

With each step forward, it often seemed that life knocked her back two.

She craned her neck and scanned the floor for the piano he'd said would await her this morning. She spotted it in a small alcove near a front window. Presumably, it was located there to draw the attention of those on the outside and lure them into the store. The Newlands were nothing if not strategic in the promotion of their business.

As instructed, she had hung her coat and hat in the fourth-floor storage room they called the employee salon and returned to the first floor.

She approached the ebony piano—a Steinway. The cabinet was polished to a satin sheen, and she ran her hand along the smooth surface. With the touch, memories assailed her. The applause. The travel. A sufficient income. Her short time here would be different from those days, and she no longer sought the lifestyle that led to her downfall.

Various pages of sheet music trembled as Phoebe placed them against the intricately carved music rack. She'd memorized the songs long ago. Regardless, it had been years since she'd played in front of an audience. She wouldn't risk forgetting the notes because of anxiety.

Seated on a padded bench, her nerves did a dance, reacting with the excitement of a child on Christmas morning.

"I trust the piano meets your standards, Mrs. Crain."

She peered up at a cheerful Spence Newland, unable to keep her fingers from stroking the surface of the keys, light enough the ivories never made a sound. Although she would have preferred a moment alone to warm up, he leaned against the curve in the case and waited. "It's a beautiful instrument."

"I saw Maura's drawing."

Phoebe had laid the paper on his desk, grateful he wasn't in his office. "She wanted to thank you for the book you sent."

"It was my pleasure." An unexpected sadness dragged down his mouth and eyelids.

Phoebe played the opening notes of one of her own compositions. Closing her eyes, she blocked out the sounds of the shoppers around her, as well as the presence of the man who had hired her. As her fingers glanced across each key, she became lost in the melody and nothing mattered but the music. Nothing mattered but the peace that filled her soul with the ebb and flow of the dulcet sounds she had created.

With the last note left to evaporate in the air, enthusiastic applause commanded her return to her surroundings.

Her eyes flew open, and the first face she saw was Mr. Newland's. Sometime during the piece, he had moved closer until he stood at the corner of the piano, near the keyboard. His face glowed with something she could only define as an admiration for what he had heard. It was the response she had hoped for on Sunday...and didn't get.

Some women would call him a fine-looking man with his kind eyes, self-assured stance, and that hint of humor that seemed to always want to wiggle his lips into an upward curve.

After her experience with Douglas, Phoebe's mother often

reminded her that "handsome is as handsome does." By the time she finished her engagement here, she would have a better feel for the depth of Mr. Newland's handsomeness.

Phoebe focused on the crowd gathered near the alcove. Exposure here might bring her new students, extending the monetary advantage of this time well beyond Christmas.

She bobbed her head at the audience.

"That was lovely, Mrs. Crain." Spencer Newland the Second broke through the crowd and leaned close to his son. "May I speak with you, Spence?"

The younger man excused himself, and the two of them walked off. They stopped several feet away while Phoebe began the next song on her list, a less complex piece. Eventually, people drifted away to carry out whatever business brought them to S. F. Newland's and Company, and new listeners halted to hear her play.

Her fingers moved of their own accord as she watched father and son in a quiet discussion. There was something so...heartrending...in the way The Third's shoulders sank as he followed his father to the elevator. At one point, Phoebe was struck with the oddest impression to go to him and provide him with encouragement.

All the more reason to mind her own business and continue playing.

Chapter Seven

S pence shut the door to his father's office. Under the circumstances, it was best no one heard their discussion.

The beautiful sound of Phoebe Crain's talent had followed them up the elevator. In his mind, he still heard the applause of the customers who had gathered to hear her play, which reassured him that he had made the right choice.

The Second leaned back in the desk chair and continued the discussion from downstairs. "Like last time, the missing articles consist mostly of small items, nothing unusual or expensive, nothing like jewelry."

Was the stock simply misplaced or miscounted in an inventory? Or was it stolen? As much as Spence wanted to believe in the two former possibilities, he and his father leaned toward the last.

"Common items, easy to resell," Spence said.

"Yes."

"Gil showed me the invoices. We can't trace what happened after delivery. Amos has no record of the stock in the warehouse."

Mentioning Gil reminded Spence that he'd never confronted his friend about his behavior with Roslyn. He'd received no complaints and had put it off.

"You and I know what this probably means, Spence."

"Chances are high that we're dealing with an employee who is a thief."

His father grimaced. "But which one?"

"I don't want to think I hired someone dishonest, someone who would betray us."

"It happens. I hope we're wrong." His father leaned over the desk. "Right or wrong, we must stop the disappearance of store merchandise. You should call in the police."

Spence played with a loose thread on the seat of his chair, trying to keep from ripping it out. While his father retained ultimate control over the store, he had been generous in allowing Spence to manage it. As such, it was Spence's responsibility to get to the bottom of the issue before it became public knowledge.

"We talked about this before, Father. If we get the police involved, word of the thefts will leak out, maybe show up in the newspapers. It won't be good exposure." And it would likely ruin his plans if Clifton Lark were to hear of it. The man would assume they...he...couldn't properly manage this store, much less new ones.

"I understand your concern, but Lark isn't so naïve as to think a business like ours doesn't come without some risk."

By now, Spence shouldn't be startled by the way The Second read his mind.

"I'm behind you in your plan to expand our interests, son, but we should think of the safety of our customers and employees. What if this thief gets bold in his efforts and decides to rob one of them? Perhaps he'll begin to steal more than petty items. Someone could get hurt."

"Father, please. Give me a little more time to find out who is behind our losses."

His father crossed his arms and studied him. "Keep me informed."

Spence rose from the chair. "I will."

He'd start his inquiry by talking with the man who delivered their merchandise, Eugene Henry. Was he in such financial straits that he had resorted to stealing?

———— ⟨∾⟩ ————

"WHY CAN'T I FIND A father at the train station?"

Phoebe slowed her steps in the hallway outside the employee salon. The little voice came from around the corner. What were Mama and Maura doing on the fourth floor?

Several beats of silence passed. With her coat draped over her arm, she waited to hear her mother's reply.

"Fathers come from lots of places, Miss Maura."

Phoebe's heart lurched. Her daughter had taken her query to The Third?

"What makes you believe you'll find someone at the railroad station?"

"Mama said that's where princes and princesses meet."

Phoebe cringed. What must Mr. Newland think of that ridiculous notion? To his credit, he didn't laugh. That didn't mean he wasn't smiling. She suspected he'd been born with a smile on his face.

"Have you ever ridden on a train?"

Phoebe had started toward them to put an end to the discussion, but Mr. Newland's voice halted her once more.

"That's how we got to Riverport, but I don't remember it much. Do you think, if I rode one again, I'd meet me a papa?"

He had tried to shift the conversation, but Maura's mind often ran like the trains—along one track. Phoebe wanted to rescue the man, but her shoes stuck to the floor, as if the soles had been nailed there.

"You miss your father, don't you?"

"I never saw him. Mama said he died before I was born."

"I'm sorry you never met him. I'm sure he was fine man."

"Mama says he was a prince."

Phoebe's lie to her daughter.

"When I ask her for another papa, she says we have to wait for God to say it's time. What does that mean?"

Phoebe pressed her hands to the sides of her burning face. Surely the man had never faced such a circumstance.

"It means your mother wants to be certain that the right man becomes your father. She wants to be confident that he'll be good to you and love you as much as she does."

And not abandon her as her real father had done. Phoebe's throat tightened.

"But my friends have fathers. I want another prince for a papa, just like in a fairy tale."

"Sometimes, Miss Maura, we can't have everything we want or the things others have."

Phoebe imagined Mr. Newland down on one knee in front of Maura, explaining things in a way she had failed to do.

"Think of it this way. Your friends don't have pretty green-and-orange-striped stockings like yours, do they?"

"No, sir. Mama helped me make them when I told her what I wanted."

"She sounds like a wonderful mother."

Spence Newland said all the right words. If Phoebe weren't careful, he would breach her defenses.

"God has different plans for each of us. He places us in different circumstances. You don't have a father like your friends, but He gave you a mother and a grandmother who love you and take care of you."

"They make me stockings."

"Yes, they make you pretty stockings."

What would Maura's life be like if she had the type of father to speak to her as Spence Newland was doing at this moment?

"Did you know the Bible says God is a father to the fatherless?"

"That's me."

Phoebe pressed her back to the hallway wall. She never thought to explain God as the perfect father to her daughter. Instead, she'd told her some absurd story about trains and princesses. Why was that?

Maybe because, no matter how badly he'd hurt her, she still held a fond memory of the first moment she saw Douglas enter the passenger car of the train bound for Chicago. He'd asked to sit next to her. She couldn't refuse such a handsome and dynamic man. A prince.

Had she known the heartache to come, she would have rejected his request.

Mr. Newland's voice broke through her thoughts. "If it's God's will that you have a new father, He'll help your mother find one for you."

"But how?"

"If she's listening, God will tell her."

"How?"

Phoebe shook her head. Yes, how?

"I'm not sure. He speaks to people in different ways. Sometimes it's in a dream or nature or a verse in the Bible. Sometimes we have to listen hard, because He speaks through a still, small voice. The point is, we must make the effort to listen, or we might miss hearing from Him."

Had that been her problem? Had she not listened hard enough to hear God speak?

"You can be my papa."

"You would be any man's ideal as a daughter, Maura, but I can't marry your mother because..."

Silence. Because why?

"We hardly know one another."

Two weeks ago, Phoebe would have said she knew all she needed to know about Spencer Newland the Third. Now, she wasn't so sure.

"What if God tells you to marry Mama?"

He laughed. "We'll cross that bridge if we ever come to it. Let's go find your mother."

Phoebe slipped back into the employee salon. Even as she reinforced her intention to maintain an emotional distance from Spence Newland, she struggled to convince herself that she meant it.

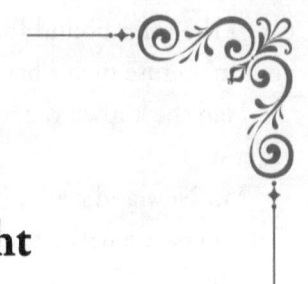

Chapter Eight

"**M**ail for you, Mr. Newland."

Spence took the envelopes from the mailroom clerk. "Thank you."

The door to his office closed again as he shuffled through the correspondence. He dropped all on his desk but the letter from Chicago.

Gripping the communication, he leaned back in his chair and stared at the envelope in his hand. He tapped it against his palm several times, listening to the soft crinkle. Each tap shouted for him to open the letter.

The Newlands had done their best to build a store to mimic establishments like Marshall Field & Company in Chicago and R. H. Macy & Company in New York. Where most of those department stores operated in large cities with six or more floors of merchandise, his father had gambled and chosen to open their store in his hometown of twelve thousand people and settled for three floors of available merchandise.

Most of the family money had been inherited or came from other ventures—a variety of them. The store was just the latest. However, the recent financial decline had taken a large bite out of the Newland family's wealth as they propped up the store's losses. A silent partner would allow them to branch out into other forms of business.

Frank Woolworth had achieved success with his five-and-dime stores in the East. Surely the Newlands could do the same in the

Midwest.

Spence continued to stare at the envelope. In his eagerness to prove himself physically and mentally strong enough to man the Newland helm, he had assured his father he would convince Lark to invest in their future.

What if he failed? What if Mr. Lark refused to take a chance on them?

Grow a backbone, Third. No one ever said succeeding in business was easy. You wanted to prove yourself, so do it.

A low growl rose in Spence's throat. The words were his, but the voice in his head belonged to his grandfather.

Spence had come a long way since the day he'd overheard The First claim that Spence's poor health would prevent him from ever running the Newland enterprises.

Over the years, he had grown that backbone and wouldn't give in to doubt now. He ripped open the envelope and pulled out an expensive sheet of notepaper.

Dear Mr. Newland,

I received your lovely gift of the cigar box and want to express my appreciation for your thoughtfulness. I find it both commendable and remarkable that you would take the time from the busyness in your day to create something for me that was both artistic and functional.

My wife also brought me your proposal for the five-and-ten-cent stores. Although I believe in your idea...

Spence drew in a deep breath and braced himself to read what his mind already knew.

...it is with deep regret that I inform you that I am unable to agree to a silent partnership in your new enterprise. However, Juliet and I wish you and your family well in your endeavor to find the proper investor.

Yours truly,

Clifton Lark

Spence dropped the letter on his desk. Well, that was that.

He spun the chair and faced the window behind his desk. The gray sky and buildings across the street faded to a blur. This was just the latest problem to progress at a merry march through his mind.

After speaking to the warehouse manager, who expressed ample faith in the trustworthiness of his employees, Spence had sought out Eugene and veiled his questions in routine conversation. He came away convinced the man was either an accomplished liar, or he knew nothing about their missing stock. Finally, he and Gil spent hours going over the account books and paperwork, looking for clues that the merchandise had been received but mishandled. Nothing came to light.

Thinking of Eugene reminded Spence of Maura. On Saturday an employee had found her wandering around the fourth floor in search of her mother. Since then Spence had not forgotten their talk...or her wish for a father. Poor child.

More often, though, his thoughts ran to her mother. For months he hadn't cared about her opinion of him. Sometime in the past few days, that had changed. Ridiculous when it was obvious Phoebe didn't like him or, at the least, didn't trust him.

Did these thoughts stem from Maura's question about him marrying Phoebe and becoming her father?

He turned back to his desk and dropped his elbows on the paper-covered top, his hands clenched together. He couldn't grant Maura her wish for a papa, but he easily could grant her another wish.

PHOEBE ENTERED NEWLAND'S, closed the wet umbrella, and wiped away drops that splashed on the tip of her nose. She preferred walking in snow to the bone-seeping dampness of a cold rain. Plus, the gray skies forecast snow, so it seemed she would experience both today.

Adding to her chill, the dollhouse Maura admired was no longer displayed in the front window. Had they sold it?

Her tense muscles relaxed at seeing they had moved it to a counter ahead of her. She still hadn't earned the money to purchase the dollhouse, but she still had a chance.

God, please keep it available for me.

She listened but heard no confirmation that the dollhouse would remain unsold. Why had she expected one?

In a soggy flour sack, she carried three completed scarves for her Widow's Might donation to the orphanage. She hoped the colors—bright blues, reds, and greens—would cheer the children who resided there.

Too often in the past five years, she had focused on her problems. It was nice to help better someone else's life.

On the way to the elevator, she caught herself searching for The Third, a troublesome behavior that reared its head whenever she entered the store these days.

The elevator operator opened the gate and asked her for a floor number. "Three, please."

After exiting the elevator, she stood in the midst of a department arranged to resemble a woman's dressing room. Current fashions in dresses and shirtwaists draped mannequins and hung on hangers against walls papered in a neutral color to best flaunt the merchandise. Wardrobes with their doors thrown open exposed more choices. The latest styles of velvet and feathered hats tempted her to stop and pluck them from their stands to try on.

Toward the back of the floor, women's undergarments filled display shelves and dressed more mannequins. She avoided a section with extravagant colorful, lacy corsets—once a weakness.

Someone tapped her shoulder, and she turned. Claire's smile filled her surroundings with good cheer, and her pale hair shimmered like a yellow diamond. The woman brought sunshine to any room and had proven to be one of the store's prized sales clerks. But Claire didn't belong here.

Claire's late husband, Richard Kingsley, had acknowledged his wife's interest in the field of architecture and permitted her to work in his architectural office. Shamefully, upon his death two years ago, Richard's partner made it clear that Claire was no longer welcome in the company.

For months the Widow's Might women had prayed she would find employment with an architect who would give her the same respect as a peer that her husband had given her.

Claire pointed to the sack. "The rest of them?"

Phoebe held out the scarves, but her friend waved them away. "It won't do any good to give them to me. I've been asked to take part of Mary Dobson's shift. She had an emergency and left the store. I'm afraid I'll be here for hours yet."

"Then who will deliver them?"

"I know the weather is awful, but Verbenia said she would pay for a hack if you would take them to the orphanage for us. The rest are in a crate in the employee salon, along with an envelope containing the fare."

Since she had no lesson this afternoon, Phoebe said, "I'm already wet, so I might as well."

"I'm due a short break. Would you like to go to the tea room?"

A small tea room located in a private third-floor corner invited weary customers to congregate and visit, rest and rejuvenate, then begin their shopping again. At one time, Phoebe would not have given a second thought to stopping at a restaurant or coffeehouse for refreshment. Those days had disappeared along with her marriage. "Perhaps another time."

After saying goodbye to her friend, Phoebe returned to the employee salon. Quiet sobs greeted her at the door. A woman no older than Phoebe's twenty-four years, and possibly younger, stood against the far wall, head down and shoulders quaking. She was dressed in the same dove-gray skirt and crisp white shirtwaist as Claire and all the other sales clerks working at Newland's.

Phoebe pulled a handkerchief from her pocket and offered it to the distraught woman.

A frail smile tipped the clerk's lips as she grasped the linen square and sniffled. "Thank you, ma'am. I-I couldn't find m-mine." The tears began in earnest again.

"Would you like to talk about what's troubling you?"

The woman wiped the tears pooling under her eyes. "No. No, I couldn't."

Phoebe considered picking up the box she'd come for and leaving the woman in peace, but she sensed she was needed.

"I'm not normally weepy. I'm just so tired of how he treats me, you know?" The woman's prominent chin quivered as she dabbed at bloodshot eyes in an effort to control herself.

"Who is he?"

"My husband."

"He's physically abusive?"

"No." She rubbed a wrist covered by the sleeve of her blouse. "It's the cruel things he says."

Phoebe's heart went out to the woman.

"Is there a problem, ladies?" Both women turned their attentions to the doorway, where Spence Newland stood.

The clerk stepped away. "No, sir."

His gaze shifted to Phoebe. "I thought I heard your voice, Mrs. Crain. It isn't Friday."

"I'm here for the crate." She pointed to the small table against the back wall.

His glance bounced between the two women, to the table, and back to Phoebe. Lines etched the area between his eyes. "Perhaps you'll tell me what's going on."

"It's not my place to say." Phoebe strode toward the table. "I'll take what I came for and leave you two to speak in private."

"Roslyn?"

When Phoebe turned around, he had blocked the doorway, spread his feet, and crossed his arms. Evidently, no one was leaving until he received an answer.

Chapter Nine

Phoebe studied the blonde she had seen behind the perfume counter. Her husband was the chief accountant for the store. She only knew that because he had stopped to listen to her play once and introduced himself. Although he was friendly, Phoebe had found his manner too smooth for her taste.

Roslyn's jaw tightened a moment before she responded to her employer. "Gil and I argued. That's all."

Mr. Newland's stance softened. "I don't know what is going on with the two of you, but this can't continue, not in the store."

A spark of defiance darkened the woman's watery blue eyes. "Perhaps you should tell that to your friend."

"I'll talk to him." He stood aside, his eyes sympathetic. "In the meantime, I'm sure they're waiting for you on the floor."

Roslyn wiped the tears away and held up the handkerchief. "I'll return this later, Mrs. Crain."

"Take your time."

She flashed a quick smile of appreciation at Phoebe and walked past her employer.

Mr. Newland ran a hand down his face, then inhaled and released a harsh breath. "What does one do about two people—friends—who seem unsuitable?"

Assuming he asked a rhetorical question, Phoebe packed the crate with the scarves she'd made, then lowered the lid. She turned with the box and bumped into him.

"What's in there?"

She stepped back. "Handmade scarves and mittens for the children at the orphanage."

"Do you mind if I see them?"

Though she silently asked why, she said, "If you'd like."

He set the crate back on the table, opened it, and peered at the contents. He felt around and accomplished a thorough inspection with understated movement. It was strange behavior for a man who only wanted a look.

He closed the box. "I'm sure each child will appreciate the gift. Let me carry this for you."

"It's not heavy, and I don't want to keep you from your work."

He lifted the container from the table and started for the door. She seized the envelope she'd set alongside the crate and followed.

"I'll have my carriage brought around and drive you."

Her chest might well have been encased in concrete for the difficulty she had in breathing. What made wealthy young men think she could be maneuvered into whatever deeds fit their whims? "Mr. Newland, I have money for a hack and am perfectly capable of making the trip alone."

"Phoebe, the weather is awful, and I have the time to see you there and back safely."

She hated hearing him use her given name, because it roused an impatience in her to hear it again.

"That's all you want?" The words rumbling through her mind snapped from her mouth, but it was too late to tone them down.

"What else?" His eyebrows formed a deep V shape. They jumped the moment he understood. He shook his head. "I've conducted myself as a gentleman around you, treating you with the respect I would show any woman. Why must you strike out at me like a hissing cat slapping at the nose of a friendly dog?"

His eyes flashed, and she expected him to drop the box into her hands and walk away. Instead he said, "I'm not sure what about me has gotten your goat, but whatever it is, I find your attitude uncalled for and unfair."

A ripple of doubt cracked the concrete in Phoebe's chest. Dare she believe he wanted nothing but friendship from her? Had she become so cynical in the past five years that she couldn't accept a man's help without believing he had an ulterior motive?

Relentless rain beat the roof like drumsticks on the surface of a kettledrum. To accept a ride from him was a terrible idea. Terrible.

Then again, she'd need to search for a hack. In the rain. In the cold rain.

When Spence Newland walked down the hallway with the crate, Phoebe trailed behind. She would let him drive her. But she would keep up her guard.

SPENCE PLACED THE CRATE on the floor under the carriage seat while Phoebe waited in a dry location under the store's awning.

Why had he volunteered for this trip when he had a desktop covered with work, a thief to find, and a stubborn investor he'd decided not to give up on?

Thankfully, the box contained only knitted winter clothing accessories and not store merchandise. He'd already accused Phoebe of extortion, which he regretted. A few minutes ago, he'd worried about needing to accuse her of theft.

He could accurately accuse her of distrusting him. It only made him more determined to find out why.

Spence accompanied Phoebe to the carriage and helped her inside. Seated next to her, he prodded the gelding into a brisk walk along the sloppy rain-soaked street.

They headed south and crossed the bridge spanning the river. Rain struck the canopy and dripped down the sides, spattering onto his left sleeve. It darkened portions of the gelding's copper coat and left the road a rutted and puddled mess.

They had traveled a mile from town without saying a word. To fill the discomforting quiet, he asked, "Did you make all those scarves and mittens?"

"Only a few. The rest come from the other members of Widow's Might."

There was that name again. "I'm not familiar with the organization. What do you do?"

"We're not an organization, just a group of friends who meet socially once a week. Occasionally, we take on charitable projects."

"Everyone is widowed?"

She straightened a skirt that didn't need straightening, and they advanced a good thirty yards on their journey while Spence waited for an answer. "Yes."

Pithy and to the point. He'd anticipated a bit more explanation but let it go. They fell back into silence.

Minutes later, Spence turned off a country lane and onto the drive that led to the Bethel Children's Home. Fallow fields lined each side. Here the boys were taught to plant and harvest. Outbuildings housed machinery that they learned to use and repair. The girls learned to can, cook, and care for a home. At the same time, they all attended school. The home provided everything the children needed to become competent adults. Everything but a family.

He halted the horse and stared through a light drizzle at the large two-story building. The whitewash on the plain wood-frame exterior had faded to a dull gray, adding a greater somberness to the structure's purpose.

"My family has supported this orphanage for years, but this is the first time I've visited. I should have made it a point to come here before now. I imagined the place as a clean, pleasant home for children who are happy and healthy. I wasn't expecting it to look this...dismal."

"The small staff does their best with the needs of the children who live here. It's relatively clean, but I'm afraid it isn't any less gloomy inside."

A rusty-haired boy of about twelve years opened the door. His clothing hung on him like Maura's coat had hung on her. The sight was like a punch to Spence's ribs. "Do you know him?"

"No. I've only been here a couple of times."

Someone must have said something, because the boy looked behind him and moved away from the door.

They were greeted by the administrator, Mr. Jernigan, a balding, lean-framed man, haggard looking, yet with a twinkle in his blue eyes. In the background, children talked and laughed, though not in a raucous manner. The floor above them creaked with several pairs of footsteps.

Spence handed Mr. Jernigan the crate.

"Thank you, Mr. Newland. It's a pleasure to meet you." He turned to Phoebe. "Please thank your friends, Mrs. Crain. God has provided you ladies with charitable hearts. The children will be delighted."

Even with a less-than-stellar financial state these days, Spence had the ability to outgive Phoebe Crain and the Widow's Might ladies every day of the week. But these children needed something the Newland's money couldn't buy them and the widows couldn't provide—mothers and fathers to raise and love them.

With nothing to do while Jernigan discussed the contents of the crate with Phoebe, Spence explored his surroundings.

Phoebe was right. The house was neat but dark. They could use more lamps, newer and brighter wallpaper, and window curtains of a lighter shade and material. He shivered in the chilly dampness. They could use more heat.

The boy he had seen at the door peered around the corner of a wall. Spence stepped closer. "My name is Mr. Newland. What's yours?"

Nothing.

"Jamie don't talk to strangers." A towheaded girl about nine years old reached for the boy's hand. "He talks to me though."

It was good to learn the boy was capable of speech. "I hope you won't consider me a stranger next time, Jamie." Next time? He made it sound as if he planned to return soon. He scanned the room again. Maybe he would.

"We're finished with our business, Mr. Newland."

He looked around the drawing room one more time. "I am, too, Mrs. Crain."

He had been too forward in using her given name earlier. Try as he might, he couldn't drum up any remorse. He liked the name Phoebe. Unless she grew testy, he planned to keep using it.

WHILE THEY WERE INSIDE the orphanage, the rain had turned to snow, which added another layer of treachery to the road's surface.

Spence huddled deeper in his coat, glad for the top over the carriage. He kept the gelding at a gentle pace. Flakes landed on the animal's back like invading soldiers. They promptly disappeared, defeated by the weapon of a warmer body.

They reached the main road, and Phoebe asked, "Why did you inspect the contents of the crate?"

He thought he'd been subtle in his search. "Promise you won't get upset?"

"Yes."

She was a lovely liar. "I was looking for missing inventory."

Phoebe stared at him—glared, really. "You thought I was a thief sneaking something out of the store?"

"Ah, ah." He waggled a finger at her. "You promised."

She freed a dainty huff. "Is it a lot of merchandise?"

"It has added up."

"This has happened more than once?"

"Three times that we know of." He frowned. "Apparently I'm no Sherlock Holmes, because I'm stymied as to how it's being done. No one has provided any useful information."

"You suspect an employee."

His eyebrows arched. "How did you know?"

"Don't tell anyone, but I've read a couple of the detective's cases." Her lips twitched, as if cracking a full smile meant betraying whatever vow she'd taken to remain aloof toward him. "Now that I know, I'll keep watch during my hours at the store."

Spence's grip tightened on the reins. "That's a nice offer, Phoebe, but I'd prefer you not get involved. We don't know what kind of person we're dealing with."

"Have you contacted the police?"

He should. He'd failed in his own investigation. "Not yet."

"Why not?"

"It's complicated and could have an adverse effect on our future plans."

The snow changed to a light rain again.

"Are you closing the store?"

"What made you jump to that conclusion?"

"I may know little about what it takes to run a company, but I do know it's been a hard few years for businesses."

"We're not closing." Spence sighed. He probably shouldn't speak of it, but he couldn't afford a rumor of the store's demise spreading. "Can you keep a confidence?"

"Of course." Her tone said she considered his question unnecessary.

"We're planning to expand by opening five-and-ten-cent stores."

"You set aside the area in Newland's to test the feasibility of your plan?"

He grinned. "You know more about business than you've admitted. You're right. Things have been difficult these past years. There was a time when we could expand with the help of a bank loan.

Unfortunately, bankers are still stingy with their money, so we need an investor—a silent partner. We thought we'd chosen the perfect man, but he declined."

"He was the one to receive the cigar box?"

"Yes." Talented and intuitive. Why couldn't that intuition tell her to trust him as he was trusting her by revealing the information about Lark?

"I'm sorry. I tried to return it the night you came for it. You'd already ridden off."

He jerked on the reins, caught by surprise. Once he'd settled the prancing gelding, he said, "It doesn't matter. His wife had left town before I learned of the mix-up. I shipped it to him and received a polite letter of appreciation."

"But you won't give up on him?"

"No. If he hears news of our thefts, I'm afraid all hope will be lost."

"Is it possible he isn't the right man to invest in your idea?"

Spence shrugged. "Clifton Lark has a reputation for integrity, which is important to us."

"In that case, you should take you own advice."

"What advice?"

She winced. "I overheard your conversation with Maura last Saturday."

He chuckled. "Why didn't you make yourself known? I could have used your support."

"You were doing fine, and I didn't want to interrupt."

"Your daughter asks hard questions."

His comment won a tiny smile from her. "She's relentless with them. I wish I had thought to tell her about God in the form of a father to the fatherless."

"What advice did I give her that I should heed?"

"You told her God would help me find her a father if it was His will. You also said I'd need to listen to Him. Doesn't that apply to you and your investor? If it's God's will that you partner with someone, do you believe He'll help you find the right person? Or were those only pretty words to ease a little girl's disappointment?"

Spence couldn't remember the last time he had relied on God for direction. What he'd said to Maura had come naturally. He believed it...and often failed to heed his own counsel.

"I also remember telling Maura she had a wonderful mother."

Phoebe turned away, seemingly uncomfortable with the praise, but he refused to take it back.

Something flashed in his peripheral vision.

"Spence, look out!"

Chapter Ten

Phoebe seized the side rail as the back wheels of the carriage slid into a shallow, muddy ditch. Even with a death grip, she bounced across the seat until her hip met Spence's.

He worked to guide the horse from the mud and onto the road. The animal tugged and pranced while the buggy rocked at a dangerous tilt. At long last, the horse stood still. Its sides heaved, but its last steps had stabilized the carriage.

Spence relaxed the reins, though the fingers entwined with the leather trembled. Understandable. She also quaked inside.

He turned to her. "Are you all right?"

"I-I'm..." She used the rail to pull to the other side of the seat. "Yes, I'm fine."

"I'm sorry, Phoebe. Had I paid more attention to driving, I might not have lost control when that deer jumped out in front of us."

"I'm sure my shout didn't help." She adjusted the hat that had knocked sideways when she'd slid into him. "I am thankful the carriage didn't tip."

Phoebe pressed a hand to her chest as a giggle erupted, expanded, then burst into laughter.

"What's funny?"

He eyed her as if she were losing her mind, which brought more bizarre laughter. Tears blurred her vision, but she couldn't stop. "Which of us do you think received the greatest fright? Was it us, the deer, or the poor horse?"

He cracked that inevitable smile. He really did have a nice smile. "I'd guess it was mutual terror."

"Me too." Phoebe fought to catch her breath and wiped the tears away. "I'm sorry. I don't know what got into me."

"Don't be sorry. I enjoyed it. The laughter, I mean."

Lightheaded over the deep rumble in his voice, she looked away, breaking the connection sparked by his steady gaze.

He climbed down from the carriage. "I'll see what I can do to get us back on the road."

His quiet words and gentle hand soothed the spooked horse and coaxed him forward. The buggy jerked but went nowhere. His well-polished shoes squished through mud as he trudged around the vehicle and examined the wheels. The carriage shook. A moment later, he unhitched the animal.

"What are you doing, Mr. Newland?"

"I preferred Spence." He led the horse to her side of the buggy. "I don't know much about these things, but it looks like something broke when we hit the ditch. Do you ride?"

She stilled. "You mean...him?"

His lips twitched. "It's either him or I tote you piggyback."

He wasn't serious about either choice. Was he?

She eyed the animal, and her heart rate sped. "Let's wait for someone to come along and help."

"We've passed one or two wagons this afternoon. We could wait for hours. It will be dark soon, and the temperature will drop. We have no choice, Phoebe."

She studied the horse. All she could think about was Douglas's fate. "I've never been atop a horse in my life."

"I'll walk beside you. I won't let you fall."

"You'll walk and leave me alone up there?" The image of a bolting horse alarmed her. What if he couldn't hang on to the animal?

"I'll never let you fall, Phoebe. Never." Spence held out his hand, while his stare locked on to hers. "Trust me."

The intensity in his eyes begged for more than faith in his ability to keep her on a horse. So much more.

Run. Run. Run.

Like the deer, she longed to escape the danger in her path.

Phoebe lifted her arm but hadn't the courage to reach out. Did she dare place her trust in another wealthy young man with the power to bring about a fall?

Her fingers stretched, then curled. Stretched and curled. What would happen if she turned her back on his appeal?

For the rest of her life, she would remain a slave to the memory of a selfish, merciless *boy* who had no right to instill an ounce of guilt and cynicism in her.

He speaks to people in different ways. Sometimes it's in a dream or nature or a verse in the Bible. Sometimes we have to listen hard, because He speaks through a still, small voice.

Spence's words to Maura echoed in her ears.

Tell me what to do.

She listened for that voice and released a shaky breath.

A cold gust whipped a loose strand of hair over her face. She brushed it from her eyes, but it persisted.

She drew in a breath and placed her hand on Spence's palm, letting his fingers enclose hers in a man's grip.

SPENCE EYED THE CLOCK, wadded another piece of paper, and tossed it across the workbench. Two hours in his workshop with little progress.

He hadn't eaten since breakfast and knew better than to miss a meal. He'd tempted his health enough through that miserable trip to and from the children's home.

Miserable? Memorable was more like it.

Phoebe had held quite an inner argument with herself as he'd waited for her to decide whether she could rely on him. Trust won out. Now it was up to him to never violate that trust.

The wind howled outside. It whistled under the door and through tiny cracks at the side windows. At least the old shed had a nice potbelly stove to warm both his cold hands and coffee.

While pulling a blank sheet of paper from those he kept on hand, Spence relived hearing the ache in Maura's voice, seeing the hope when she asked if he could be her papa. How could he quit when he wished to make her dollhouse special, something she would be proud to keep for years? His gift would never take the place of a father, but her mother believed it would brighten her holiday, so he would do his part.

He paused with the tip of the pencil touching the paper. Christmas was fast approaching. How would he finish when he hadn't made up his mind how to start?

At the close of the door behind him, Spence glanced over his shoulder, then dropped the pencil. He snatched the sheet of paper off the workbench, turned, and hid the drawing behind his back, away from his little sister's prying eyes.

"I thought I'd find you here," she said.

"I wasn't expecting you."

"What a greeting. Is there something wrong with wanting to see my big brother?"

"Not at all." He gave Laurie a one-armed hug. "It's good to see you."

"Let's not get too sentimental." She pulled away from him and eyed the workbench. "Are you making something new? Something for Christmas?" She waggled her eyebrows. "Something for me?"

He stepped in her way. "If it was for you, scamp, I wouldn't tell you."

She craned her neck and tried to see around him. Suspicion narrowed her eyes. "What do you have behind your back?"

Spence's hand tightened, crinkling the paper. At the same time, he shook his head. "Just an idea."

"What kind of idea?"

His sixteen-year-old sister had grown into a first-rate snoop. "You should curb that curiosity before it gets you into trouble."

"I've always been curious and lived to tell about it." She stopped in front of him and bounced up and down on her toes, her smile sly and dangerous. "A secret?"

Before he could brace himself, her hand shot around him and gained a grip on his drawing. "You'll tear it."

"Then let go so I can see." She tugged but not hard enough to rip the paper. Her glance slid toward the workbench, and she released the drawing.

Spence had forgotten the other iterations he'd cast aside and was too slow in stopping her from snatching a rejected design. He should have tossed them into the stove.

Laurie backed a safe distance away and opened the balled-up sheet of paper. She gasped. "You're drawing plans to build a house? Why? What's wrong with this one?" Confusion furrowed her forehead. "Why does it only have four rooms?"

Once his sister bit into a subject, she would chew on it until she'd swallowed the facts—all of them. He might as well confess. "Yes, I am building a house, and it only contains four rooms because it's a dollhouse."

"Are you still battling with Father over the one at the store?"

"No. This is for a little girl I've met." Spence showed her the drawing in his hand. "I haven't finished it, but what do you think?"

"I do like the cupola."

"Does the Italianate style make it appear too plain? Maybe she would prefer a Queen Anne or something in a Greek Revival."

His sister tucked her lips, trying to hold in a smile, then said, "How old is the little girl?"

"Five."

"I think this one is perfect."

"Maybe I'm in over my head. I know nothing about little girls, let alone how to decorate the inside of a dollhouse."

"We still have some scrap wallpaper and leftover linoleum from Mother's decorating frenzy last year. I'll see what I can find."

"Good idea."

"Who is she?"

He hesitated to give too many details but said, "Her name is Maura."

"Maura? Is she related to the woman Wally told me is playing piano at the store?"

"Wally?" She called the nineteen-year-old boy Wally?

"Don't be so pompous, Spence. He's a sweet boy."

"Yes, he is a boy."

His sister snapped her fingers.

"Really, Laurie? Mother should take you in hand and teach you to act like a lady."

"I've seen her do the same."

That was true.

"Mrs. Crain is the one you accompanied to the orphanage yesterday."

"How do you know about that?" He raised his hand. "Wait. Wally."

She showed him the tip of her tongue. "No. All of Mother's biddy friends are buzzing with the tale."

Wonderful.

"Too bad about the wheel."

Was there nothing about the incident the imp hadn't ferreted out? "Which biddy provided *that* information?"

"You both arrived in town a muddy mess, then went your own ways, pretending you hadn't traveled together. That, big brother, I saw with my own eyes."

At Phoebe's request, he had helped her off the horse before

reaching the bridge. What a time they'd had!

Phoebe Crain was a constant surprise, as was his sister. "The Pinkertons could use you."

"What a fun thought." Laurie focused on the finger she ran along the edge of the workbench. "I've heard she's a widow."

"Who?"

"You know very well who."

Something dastardly brewed in his sister's devious mind. "And?"

"I think it's sweet of you to want to give her daughter a gift." Laurie's voice was filled with an overabundance of cheer. "I'd be glad to help you."

His eyes narrowed, as they often did around Laurie. "Why?"

"Since you moved into your house, I hardly see you anymore." She pouted. "You don't want to spend time with me?"

He ran a thumb and forefinger down his mustache. He knew his sister well enough to be sure to stay on his toes around her. He also knew she would pester him until she got her way. "Fine. While we're working on the dollhouse, you and I will discuss Wally."

The pout turned to a cunning grin. "I find Mrs. Crain a more interesting subject."

Inwardly, Spence agreed. Outwardly, he frowned. "I'm hungry. Let's get something to eat, then we'll get to work on Maura's dollhouse."

VERBENIA'S TWO-WHEELED cart bounced across the bridge as she and Phoebe traveled to the children's home to deliver the remaining items made by the ladies in their circle. Unlike Phoebe's last visit, the sun shone, the clouds were tinged with blue as opposed to gray, and the road, though rutted, was dry.

As they passed the spot where Spence Newland's carriage had slid into the ditch, Phoebe's attention slid in that direction. All that remained were hoofprints, deep grooves from the wheels...and Phoebe's fledgling trust.

"Is that where Mr. Newland's carriage left the road?" The cart horse picked up his pace, and Verbenia eased back on the reins. "Careful, Diamond."

"You heard?" How widespread was the gossip?

"Even in a town of this size, word goes around with the speed and ease of a spinning wheel at the fair." Verbenia winked. "Especially if it involves an eligible bachelor and a young widow."

Obviously, Phoebe's precaution had not kept the situation from turning into tittle-tattle.

"What do you think of him?"

Verbenia chortled. "As an employer, a human being, or a man?"

"As a human being, of course." Phoebe wasn't ready to be acquainted with the man.

Her friend's lips puckered and chin jutted as she thought. "For me, what stands out about The Third is his patience and thoughtfulness. On his way through the store, he'll stop to help a customer if need be or chat with a clerk. He's never too far above others to be of service. In my opinion, he takes after his father in that regard—a true gentleman."

He could easily have taken advantage of the situation during their plight on the road. On the contrary, he'd been nothing but gracious and...a true gentleman.

"Why the interest, Phoebe?" With a touch as soft as her voice, Verbenia guided the cart horse onto the long drive to the orphanage. "When we visited his house together, I felt a chill between you two."

"A few days before, we'd had a slight disagreement."

"I didn't realize you knew one another well."

Phoebe shrugged. "We'd met once or twice. Since I work for him now, I'm interested in how he's viewed by those who know him better."

Verbenia halted the horse in front of the orphanage and turned toward her. "I've given you my opinion. However, I will add my certainty that he's no more perfect than either of us. Anything further, you should discover for yourself."

They climbed out of the cart, and Phoebe lifted the box from where it had ridden between her feet. The same boy who'd greeted them last time opened the door. Did he stand watch, waiting for a loved one to return? What a heartbreaking disappointment for him.

"Hello, Jamie. Is Mr. Jernigan here?"

He nodded and stood aside for them to enter. While they waited in the drawing room for the administrator, Phoebe inspected her surroundings, which were warmer and less gloomy than on her other visits. "There's something different about this room."

Verbenia looked around. "I believe the last time I was here there were only two lamps. I see"—she pointed as she counted—"one, two, three more."

"They're not lit, yet it's brighter in here." Phoebe glanced around. "The draperies are different too."

"Yes. That dark and heavy velvet is gone." Verbenia stroked the silky and cheerful material in a floral brocade. "They're thick enough to hold in the warmth but add some light. I've seen these before."

"Good afternoon, ladies." Mr. Jernigan entered the room. "It's probable you saw the draperies at your workplace, Mrs. Jensen. After his visit last week, Mr. Newland sent us a number of items he felt were necessary for the comfort and well-being of our children."

Phoebe's flesh tingled. "Mr. Newland did this? The Third?"

"Yes indeed. He visited us again yesterday to see that everything had been delivered satisfactorily." Mr. Jernigan gestured to a table with a new lamp and a stack of books. "As I told him, this room has become a popular place for reading. We've also received more than enough firewood for the winter, as well as the promise of new paint for the outside come spring. Next week we'll receive a new stove. We've praised God for the man's generosity, and we thank you, too, Mrs. Crain."

"Me?"

"You were responsible for bringing him and showing him our

needs."

"I must be honest, Mr. Jernigan. Mr. Newland volunteered to drive me here."

"Then perhaps we should say the Lord brought you both that day."

As they climbed back into the cart a few minutes later, Verbenia asked, "May I ask you a question, Phoebe?"

"Yes." She needn't answer.

"Has your judgment of Mr. Newland been colored by your experience with Maura's father?"

Phoebe's chest constricted. "What do you know about that?"

"Just what little I've observed. Whenever the other women talk about their husbands and compare their lives with them, you remain silent. You never speak of Maura's father. I don't recall hearing you mention his name."

Phoebe twisted her hands. The woman was too perceptive, but that perception often helped others. "His name was Douglas, and you are right. I don't want to talk about him."

"Then we won't." Verbenia stilled Phoebe's hands. "Nevertheless, I would caution you to base your opinion of people on an assessment of their character as individuals, not on any predetermined bias you hold against someone else."

She had already learned through this trip that the hope for her newfound faith in Spence ran deep. It ran through the hole in her trust created the day Douglas announced his betrayal. It ran to join the voice inside that urged her to forgive. It ran to smother the blame that had tossed Spence Newland into the same batch of rotten apples that Maura's father occupied.

And it was headed straight for her heart.

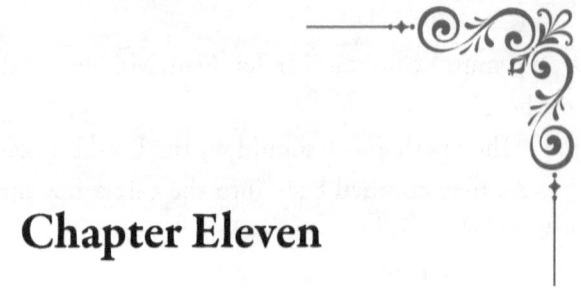

Chapter Eleven

B *ored.*
The word jumped out at Spence the moment he stepped foot inside the Davidson home. By the time he left this soirée, he'd require suspenders to hold his eyelids up.

Christmas was right around the corner. He should be home working on his latest project—possibly his most worthy project to date. He would be if events like this weren't expected of him.

Gilt-embossed wallpaper and oil paintings framed by gold-painted wood surrounded him. Crystal prisms hung from a gold-plated gas chandelier and sparkled like Queen Victoria's diamonds. Shiny golden and brass decorative pieces sat on gold-trimmed furnishings. At any time, he expected to see an old, bedraggled miner tug a donkey laden with prospecting tools across the expansive foyer.

The Davidsons wanted to ensure everyone understood their position in Riverport's pecking order.

"Good evening, Mr. Newland."

"Good evening, Mrs. Davidson. Pardon my tardiness."

"Not necessary. We know how busy you are at this time of year."

Quiet conversations took place in the drawing room to his right. He handed a servant his coat and hat and paused outside the room to observe the dozen occupants gathered in small groups, talking and laughing.

In their twenties and early thirties, they had dressed in the required evening clothes—the men in dark coats, white waistcoats, and white ties and the women in satin and velvet gowns of various hues, the short sleeves puffed like fabric balloons. Flowery and spicy scents of perfumes and hair tonics hung in the air.

Rows of chairs and sofas filled the room for the pre-supper entertainment. He often found the company of many of his peers tiresome. Added to his exasperation, these gatherings were a doorway to any number of illnesses at this time of year.

Forget the etiquette. He'd call for his coat and hat. He started to turn and brushed against Mary Alice's arm.

"Hello, Third." The daughter of his hostess inspected him with heavy eyelids and a down-turned mouth that rarely changed direction. Although too forbidding for him, her features lent her a certain solemn intelligence that some men would find attractive.

After slipping her arm through his, she guided him into the room and leaned unbecomingly close to whisper, "I shouldn't be so forward, but will you offer to be my supper escort? Mother has hinted at pairing me with someone dreadful."

"It will be my pleasure."

Her cheekbones glowed golden in the nearby lamplight. "Now that we are all here, except poor Josephine, we can begin the entertainment soon. The poor girl would have come tonight, but you know the capriciousness of her husband."

Mary Alice's gossip was like the bite of a viper. Spence had no doubt she would volunteer any information he didn't ask to hear, so he steered her to a topic less chin wagging—the upcoming holiday. After a proper interval, he excused himself with the necessity to greet other acquaintances.

While half listening to his friends, he scanned the far end of the room and recognized the evening's pianist. He'd had no idea whom the Davidsons had hired. A weight lifted from his mood.

Phoebe stood with two other women and looked stunning in a gown of black satin and sequins—a remnant from bygone days? Her expertly coiffed dark hair rivaled the styles of the other women in the room. He could well imagine her gracing a concert stage.

Spence denied his impatience and started toward her with a dawdling stride. He'd almost reached his goal, when Mary Alice glided to the front of the room near the piano. She clapped the tips of her fingers together several times in an elegant call for attention. "Ladies and gentlemen." Content to see all eyes focused on her, she said, "My parents and I invited you here this evening to enjoy a musical performance by an artist on the piano, a woman renowned for her talent."

Spence found a chair on the front row as Phoebe moved to the side while waiting to be introduced.

Once her guests were settled in the seats provided for them, Mary Alice said, "May I present Miss Phoebe Langford."

Langford?

Phoebe's stony glance hit Spence like a rock from a slingshot. He shook his head, silently assuring her he had said nothing. At the same time, he thought her reaction was a bit overblown. What difference did it make if people knew the name she performed under?

"Please welcome the Little Darling of the Ivories," Mary Alice said. While Phoebe hesitated, Mary Alice smirked, as if she'd achieved a victory.

What did she know about Phoebe that he didn't?

At the polite applause, Phoebe collected herself and sat at the piano, giving Spence a full view of her profile from the front row of seats. Mary Alice occupied the chair next to him.

Even though Phoebe's back was as straight as a plumb line and her shoulders stiff, her fingers floated across the keys in the tranquil way placid waves lapped in and out along the shoreline. The longer she played, the more she visibly relaxed, presumably lost in the music that moved her as much as it did Spence.

Mary Alice broke the spell when she whispered, "She's quite

talented. Don't you agree?"

"Quite."

"Mother recognized her at the store. Don't you wonder what else Miss Langford hides in addition to her identity?"

"Perhaps she prefers her married name because she wants privacy."

"And perhaps you shouldn't be gullible."

Gullible? Spence ground his molars and recalled the suspicion on Phoebe's face when she looked at him. The last thing he would do was betray her confidence. "It wasn't fair of you to ambush her, Mary Alice."

"Ambush her? Don't be silly. Performers thrive on recognition. Can you imagine my surprise when Mother informed me of having seen one of our own perform on a concert stage?" Mary Alice directed her dialogue to Spence, but her gaze never left Phoebe. It reminded him of a wolf staring down its prey. The mental image curled the toes inside Spence's new shoes.

Phoebe performed for another forty-five minutes while everyone in the room sat enraptured. Afterward, she turned to the audience and asked, "Does anyone have a request?"

"I do." Mary Alice stood. "I request a duet between you and Mr. Newland." She faced Spence and clapped her hands, encouraging him to accept. The others did the same.

This wasn't his first time to be asked to play during an evening out, and declining such an invitation was considered rude. He strode to the front of the room as one of the guests placed a chair next to Phoebe's stool.

"What is your choice, Mr. Newland?"

To leave, right now...with you.

A spark of rebellion struck him. "Let's liven up the party, shall we? 'Camptown Races,' Mrs. Crain."

She blinked. "'Camptown Races?'" She shot a glance at Mary Alice and whispered, "That particular tune isn't appropriate for the setting."

"Are you familiar with the music?"

"I am, but—"

"Then let's play it."

A tiny smile tipped her lips. "If you insist."

"I do."

She placed her fingers on the keys. "Are you sure you can keep up, Mr. Newland?"

"I'll do my best." He grinned. "Shall we?"

He waited as she played the introduction, then he joined in. As their fingers bounced on the keys, the others gathered around the piano.

Toes tapped the floor and hands clapped to the lively rhythm. Guests began to sing. The whole room reverberated with the sounds of sopranos and tenors and basses.

Phoebe sped up the tempo, and Spence worked hard to keep up. She laughed when he matched her note for note.

With the last note, her hands stilled, but Spence kept playing, adding his own flair of creativity to the end. As he grazed the ivories, his shoulder brushed hers. His right hand came to rest alongside her left, both warm with the exertion. He couldn't stop his fingers as they crept over hers and squeezed. The pleasure he'd noted in her expression moments before underwent a slow but dramatic change. Not quite fearful, not quite confident. Poised yet tentative.

He might well be wearing blinders. His eyes took in nothing to the left and nothing to the right, only what was before him. Only Phoebe. Just like that day in the carriage when they'd laughed over the near miss with the deer. He might have stared at her for hours that afternoon had she not looked away.

"What an interesting performance." Mary Alice continued to clap after the others had stopped.

He didn't speak fluent sarcasm. Nevertheless, Spence heard it in her voice.

Phoebe pulled her hand away. His dropped onto the keyboard to a jarring middle C.

A rosy hue stained her cheeks and added additional force to the pounding of his pulse. For several beats, he concentrated on a plant stand with its hairy fern, the shadow behind it that was created by a well-lit lamp, the wavering light—anything to calm the hot rush through his veins.

He stood and graced Phoebe with a slight bow, then loomed over Mary Alice, who had never left her seat. "It was an honor to play with someone with such immense talent. Thank you for the opportunity."

Although hard to tell from her normal expression, he thought he detected a scowl.

Mrs. Davidson announced supper. He bent his elbow and held it out. "Are you ready, Mary Alice?"

She wrapped her arm around his and held on tight. "Be careful, Spence."

"In what way?"

"Miss Langford has designs on you."

"I hardly think Mrs. Crain concerns herself with me." Spence placed his hand on Mary Alice's arm and led her away as the rest of the guests followed. He refrained from peering over his shoulder to see who led Phoebe into the dining room.

"Don't be naïve. I noticed the way she watched you when you walked in and while you spoke with our friends. Believe me—she has set her sights on you. You know the reputation of performers. I won't sit idle and see you become involved with a woman of dubious character."

Dubious character? The vein in Spence's temple throbbed as he pulled out Mary Alice's chair. "In that case, I must take care to watch her too."

Her blue eyes darkened, and her normally dour expression turned peevish.

Chapter Twelve

*W*hat a windbag.

Throughout the meal, the gentleman assigned as Phoebe's supper companion—his name escaped her—had droned on about his new golf clubs, his position in his father's company, his family's electric lights. His this. His that. Would he never close his mouth except to chew?

She glanced down the table and caught Spence watching her. She had never considered him exceptionally attractive...until tonight. Tonight something changed. It wasn't simply the evening clothes. It was something—

"Mrs. Crain."

Phoebe squeaked and dropped her fork on the china. She closed her eyes and placed her hand against her throbbing chest. Opening her eyes revealed everyone's stare aimed in her direction.

Her companion said, "I apologize, ma'am. I didn't mean to startle you."

"I'm afraid my mind wandered, Mr...." She mumbled nonsense and hoped he assumed she'd said his name.

Everyone resumed their conversation and dining, except Spence. He sported a subtle grin.

She turned to the gentleman beside her. "What were you saying, sir?"

"I was talking about..."

Phoebe's ears vibrated with the hum of his voice. Every few

seconds, she provided a polite but vague nod.

For the pay the Davidsons promised her this evening, she would put up with a time of tedium. This night alone would provide Maura a dollhouse and more.

Three weeks ago Phoebe would have scorned the suggestion of playing for a private musicale. Spence's kindness and Verbenia's advice that everyone deserved to be judged on their own merit had prompted her to rethink her attitude...and her selfishness.

She had allowed her mother and daughter to live in near poverty for five years to satisfy the fearful bitterness inside her, when more nights like this one could have provided them with a comfortable life.

At the same time, since her arrival, Phoebe had sensed an antagonism in Miss Davidson. The woman didn't introduce her as Phoebe Langford only to impress her guests. It was malicious. How had she found out?

Then Miss Davidson had added the absurd title given to Phoebe based on her young age—*the Little Darling of the Ivories*. A sneer had accompanied each word the woman spoke.

What had Phoebe done to anger her?

Now that her identity had been revealed, how long would it take the people of Riverport to start digging into her past?

THE DAVIDSONS' GUESTS prepared to leave, and Spence intended to join them, until Mary Alice latched on to him. She dragged him to the foyer to say goodbye as though they shared host duties. It took fortitude not to wince at the viselike grip clamped around his hand. He would never have imagined the strength in those fingers.

The plea to escort her in to supper. The irritability. The possessiveness in her hold.

He wasn't thickheaded. Whatever had taken place between him and Phoebe must have rattled any misunderstanding Mary Alice had that he was interested in her as more than a friend.

Phoebe was the last to leave. He suspected she delayed in order to be paid for her services. The three of them stood in the foyer with Mary Alice's mother.

In a voice as smooth as the richest chocolate, Mary Alice said, "That was quite a rainstorm a couple of weeks ago."

Spence's muscles tensed. She never mentioned anything as mundane as the weather without an ulterior motive. "Yes, it was."

"Not something anyone should be caught out in."

"Is it true that your carriage bogged down in the mud, Mr. Newland?" Mrs. Davidson eyed him as if expecting to hear a lie.

Rumor was a popular sport no matter the circles one ran in.

He and Phoebe owed no one an explanation, but an attempt to hide the truth would ricochet and cause more damage.

"I'm afraid we chose an appalling day to do a good deed, didn't we, Mrs. Crain?"

Phoebe accepted her coat from the servant who brought it. "Appalling. While I'm thankful for your kindness in offering to drive me, I should have waited for a better day to deliver the Widow's Might gifts to the children. It was selfish of me to inconvenience someone in your important position." Despite the remorseful words, there was a slight satisfaction in Phoebe's voice.

"Not at all, Mrs. Crain. The children deserved to receive their gifts."

Another pout dragged Mary Alice's lower lip to her chin. "Poor Spence. It's a wonder you didn't catch a dreadful cold and be confined again."

He bit his tongue and tasted blood.

DON'T LOOK AT HIM. *Don't say a word.*

Not having been paid yet, Phoebe couldn't afford to antagonize the Davidsons further.

Mary Alice had staked her claim on Spence this evening and resented his interaction with Phoebe—little as it had been. Judging by the barely restrained grimace on his face, she suspected that claim came as an unwelcome surprise to Spence.

What had Mary Alice meant by him being confined?

"Mother, I can see Miss Langford is ready to leave." Miss Davidson spoke the name as one would a curse.

She couldn't restrain herself. "It's Mrs. Crain."

A maid entered the foyer and whispered something to Mrs. Davidson. The older woman turned to her daughter. "Please see to the duty, Mary Alice. It seems there's an issue in the kitchen."

After both women walked away, Phoebe donned her coat, hat, and gloves, made sure the hall was empty, then edged closer to Spence. "I couldn't help but notice that you might be in need of a knight in black sequins, Mr. Newland."

"Please show me to your steed, Mrs. Crain, or should I show you to mine?"

"I believe yours would be more convenient, not to mention real."

Mary Alice returned and, with a deft move, slipped an envelope into Phoebe's hand, which settled the crass duty of paying her bill.

"Thank you for allowing me the opportunity to play for your guests, Miss Davidson." She turned to Spence. "I'm ready, Mr. Newland."

"Good night, Mary Alice."

The young woman's eyes narrowed. "You're leaving? With her?"

"I've promised Mrs. Crain a ride home."

She glared at Phoebe before quelling the anger for Spence. "I'd hoped to visit with you a while longer."

"It's late, and I'm sure you wouldn't want me to compromise a woman's safety."

If possible, her hostess's chin fell farther than it had all night.

Phoebe experienced a momentary regret. True, Miss Davidson had aimed darts at her during the evening. Be that as it may, Phoebe was well aware of the painful sting of rejection. She stepped outside to allow Spence to speak with Miss Davidson at the doorway.

After tucking her coat closer to ward off the cold night air that traveled down her bare neck, she walked to the carriage parked at the street. A few minutes later, she was seated beside Spence as his driver guided the carriage horse around the corner, out of sight of the Davidson house.

"You can let me out here."

"Why would I do that?" The light from the lantern on her side of the carriage cast a soft glow over the planes of his face, accentuating the hollow area of his cheek. "My comment about your safety was not an excuse to escape, Phoebe, and the offer to see you home was not made in jest."

"Oh." She drummed her fingers on her lap, replaying the "Camptown Races" tune.

He stared out the window and into the night. "I don't know what got into Mary Alice."

"Yes, you do. Jealousy is a powerful weapon in a woman's hands."

"One she wielded against you."

Phoebe didn't need to see his face to hear his outrage.

"I've never known her to be as unpleasant as she was tonight, and she's never given me a second glance."

Phoebe doubted that. He'd simply missed it. "How did she learn my identity?"

"Her mother recognized you from a performance several years ago."

"In that case, I take back the terrible thoughts I had about you."

"They weren't the first."

She laughed. "No."

"Before I left, I set Mary Alice straight. I don't dally with a woman's emotions."

Loyalty. Trustworthiness. Devotion.

Douglas could demonstrate any of the qualities when it came to getting what he wanted. Beyond that, they were foreign traits to him.

Uncomfortable with the course of the discussion, she switched topics. "I like the new draperies in the drawing room of the orphanage."

"You went back?"

"Mrs. Jensen and I made our last delivery of scarves on Tuesday. Mr. Jernigan said the new lamps have encouraged more reading."

"Children should never live in the dark."

The statement erupted with a fervor she hadn't expected and prompted the recollection of Mary Alice's comment. "When did you live in the dark, Spence?"

"What makes you ask that?"

"Other than that last comment? There was spite in Miss Davidson's remark about catching cold and being confined. She meant to get your attention. By the look I saw on your face, she succeeded."

The horse slowed from a brisk clip-clop to a plod, as if it, too, sensed her companion's sudden melancholy. "When I was a youngster, I'd get intense headaches. Migraines. When they attacked, they were incapacitating. During those times, I was confined to my bedroom with the drapes drawn and the room dark. Even without the headaches, I was a sickly child and rarely ventured from the house."

Thinking back on the strength of his hand as he'd helped her from the carriage and the power with which he'd lifted her onto the horse's back, she couldn't imagine him in poor health. Yet his childhood experience revealed why he was a health-conscious adult. "That must have been a dreadful and lonely existence."

"On more than one occasion, the doctors warned my parents of the possibility I would not survive to adulthood." His wry bark of laughter stirred the howl of a dog in a nearby yard. "The first time my mother caught me whittling with a knife, she almost keeled over. Mother didn't want me rushing my end."

"That's really not funny, Spence. I can't fathom how I would react if Maura were so ill that she might...die." Just saying the word sent a tremor through Phoebe's body. "Given your history, I'm even more grateful that you risked your health to drive me to the orphanage in the cold and snow."

"I am no longer an invalid, Phoebe!"

She flinched at the harshness of the response.

Spence shook his head. "I apologize for the outburst. I get irritable when people treat me as if I'm weak."

"That wasn't my intention."

The driver reined the horse onto her street.

"When I was fourteen, I overheard my grandfather telling my father that he should see to it Laurie married well because even if I survived, he didn't believe I'd ever be strong enough to handle the family's business affairs."

How could a grandfather give up on his grandson so easily? If necessary, Mama would fight tooth and nail to see to Maura's healing.

"From that day on I devoted myself to proper eating and hard physical training. I gained the strength I needed to prove him wrong about me." Spence shifted on the seat. "That's my deepest, blackest bruise in life, Phoebe. What is yours?"

If only hers were as innocent as his.

The driver stopped the carriage in front of her house. "It's late. My mother will be worried."

"You won't tell me?"

"No."

Spence helped her from the carriage, grasping her hand for longer than necessary. "I hope a day will come when you'll feel comfortable enough to tell me more about yourself."

"Thank you for bringing me home." She pulled her hand free and hurried up the walk before he offered to accompany her to the door.

When she reached the porch, he called her name, and she found him still standing at the side of the carriage. "Yes?"

"Will you join me at my house for lunch tomorrow? I have a surprise for you. Come alone."

"Alone?" Maybe she hadn't read him wrong after all. The tip of her tongue rolled over her lips, but moistening them did little good when her mouth had dried like the herbs hanging in the pantry. She'd had it up to her ears with men's "surprises."

"I meant nothing improper, Phoebe. There's something I want to show you." He took one step forward and stopped when she took one step back. "If it eases your mind, my sister will join us."

Another person's presence did make a difference to her. And it was lunch, not an intimate candlelit supper. Not a late-night carriage ride.

She stood mute while he waited for an answer, but what was she to say? How had she gone from scorn toward him to respect for him in less than a month?

She murmured, "Oh, Lord, what do I tell him?" There was a time when she would not have sought God's direction. Now, it came naturally.

Even in the darkness, it was evident Spence's shoulders sank. "It's all right. Good night, Phoebe." He started to climb into the carriage.

This man was trustworthy and kind. Most of all, he was not Douglas.

"Wait."

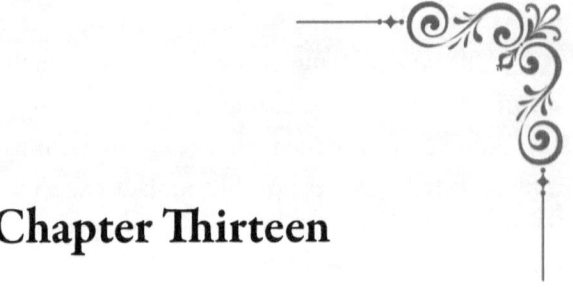

Chapter Thirteen

Phoebe raised her hand to knock on Spence's door and knocked on air.

A girl—sixteen or seventeen—stood on the other side of the open door. Wearing a replica of Spence's broad smile, she looked as if she'd been given an early Christmas present. "Please come in, Mrs. Crain. I'm Laurie Newland."

"It's nice to meet you, Miss Newland. Please call me Phoebe."

"Laurie." She led her into the drawing room and gestured to the striped sofa. "Spence will be in shortly."

The last time Phoebe had entered this room, the grand piano had filled the area near the window. Now the space gaped large and empty, awaiting the instrument's return. She hadn't expected this sadness to strike at the thought of losing the opportunity to continue playing the beautiful piano after Christmas.

She surveyed the rest of the room, observing the things nervous tension hadn't allowed the last time she visited. Not frilly or ornate, yet not too masculine and bland. From the carpet to the gas fixture hanging from the ceiling, the décor reflected comfort, good taste, and light. Like the items donated to the orphanage, nothing darkened the room, not the fabrics or the wallpaper or the wood.

Laurie sat next to her on the sofa. "My brother told me about your little girl. Maura, is it?"

"Yes. She's five."

"I'm looking forward to meeting her."

Why would she want to meet Maura?

"Has my sister talked your ear off yet, Mrs. Crain?"

Phoebe's gaze flitted to Spence as he stood in the doorway to the drawing room. Laurie cleared her throat and, with a pointed look at her brother, ran a hand over her hair. He received the message. Phoebe sucked in her cheeks as he finger-combed the unruly hair that stood up on the crown of his head and resembled the fin of a porpoise.

"It's been a busy morning."

His self-consciousness melted Phoebe's reserve.

Laurie jumped up from the sofa. "I'll tell Mrs. Rosenbach we're ready for lunch." She rushed from the room, leaving Phoebe alone with Spence.

"I apologize for my sister. She's often spontaneous in her actions."

His statement gave credence to Phoebe's suspicion that the girl's good humor typically bubbled and popped like a cream soup cooking on a hot stove. "I've only just met her, but I can see she's quite spirited...in a good way."

"I could tell you stories."

"No, you won't!" The girl's call came from somewhere outside their vision.

Spence slipped Phoebe's arm through his and laughed all the way to the dining room.

SPENCE TRIED TO CONCENTRATE on his salad, but the oil and vinegar didn't mix well with his nervous stomach. After Phoebe's hesitation in accepting his invitation last night, he'd doubted she would come.

Laurie sipped her hot tea. "Where did you learn to play the piano, Mrs. Crain?"

"Someone saw potential in me and insisted I learn."

"From there, you performed in concert halls?"

Where had she heard that information? Spence hadn't spilled those beans. "Which of Newland's employees have you been gossiping with?"

Laurie paid undue attention to her lettuce salad.

"Let me guess. *Wally.*"

His sister stuck out her tongue, then darted a glance at Phoebe and reined it in. "Yes. Wally."

Phoebe dabbed her lips with the napkin but failed to hide her amusement.

Laurie popped a piece of lettuce into her mouth, chewed, swallowed, and said, "You were going to tell us about your performances, Mrs. Crain."

"Don't pester her, young lady."

"I don't mind. Wallace was correct. Before Maura was born, I performed in front of audiences in small-town music halls on occasion."

Laurie's brows lifted. "You must have started very young."

"I began at sixteen."

"My age."

"I was too young. Such an opportunity can go to a person's head, especially when one is not fully mature." Phoebe smiled, but the words held a warning for Laurie.

His sister's voice was breathless when she asked, "Have you ever performed in New York?"

Phoebe laughed. "No, but it would be marvelous, wouldn't it?"

A screech and shouting from the kitchen interrupted the conversation.

Spence aimed a frown at his sister. "I'm sure we know what that is about."

Laurie tossed her napkin on the table and jumped from her seat. "Excuse me." She dashed from the room in the direction of the noise.

Once she'd gone, he rubbed the spot between his eyes. "Don't look so concerned, Phoebe. It's only Myron."

"Myron?"

"A few months ago, Laurie rescued a baby squirrel from the clutches of a cat and insisted upon raising him. She takes the spoiled creature everywhere with her. Every now and then, Myron escapes his cage and finds his way to the kitchen, where he enjoys the warmth of the stove. For some reason, Mrs. Rosenbach doesn't appreciate his presence."

Phoebe clucked her tongue. "How unreasonable of her."

His shoulders shook. "Isn't it?"

She pushed a lettuce leaf around her plate. "You mentioned a purpose for this invitation."

"A few weeks ago, you asked me to build Maura a dollhouse."

"A request you considered extortion."

"I was angry at the time."

"With good cause." She ran the tines of her fork through the dressing pooling on her plate. "Have you changed your mind?"

"I've not only changed my mind, I asked you here to see what I've done. What Laurie and I have done."

The hand holding the fork froze. "You've built Maura a dollhouse?"

PHOEBE FOLLOWED SPENCE into the building behind his house. He lit several lanterns until the interior shone a yellow-orange. "Let me get the stove started so we're not shivering."

She was on tenterhooks, certain this was a dream. Why had he changed his mind?

While he stuffed the stove with kindling, Phoebe inspected the well-ordered space. Handsaws, planes, chisels, and hammers hung from hooks and nails on the walls. The room smelled of lumber, paint, and wood stains. Shelves held jars of nails and screws. He had stacked scrap wood in various sizes against one wall, and numerous larger tools—many of which she couldn't name—packed strategic places throughout the building.

"You have a well-equipped shop." And the cleanliness said much about his habits.

"There are a few things I'd like to add, but I prefer to purchase them as needed."

Where would he put anything else?

If he'd had an interest in such things, Maura's father would have purchased everything at once, then let much of it sit idle or never used. Not for the first time, she asked herself what she had seen in the man.

Laurie pointed to the workbench and a large lump covered by a stained cloth. "You and Maura will adore the dollhouse, Phoebe." She placed the basket she'd carried with her on the workbench. "I brought some wallpaper remnants Mother was happy to part with. You know your daughter best, so choose whichever ones you think she'd like." She laid various wallpaper pieces alongside the basket.

Phoebe ran a finger over a deep red floral pattern. "This is lovely, but Maura is drawn to bright colors."

"I've seen her green-and-orange socks." Spence reached into the basket and pulled out a scrap of bright blue wallpaper with tiny red-and-white flowers. "How about this?"

"Perfect." Her fingers itched to remove the covering that hid the dollhouse. "May I see it?"

"Of course." He turned to his sister. "Would you like to do the honors?"

The girl hopped up and down. "Yes, I would." She yanked the cloth off.

The sight of the dollhouse stole Phoebe's breath. Finally her daughter would receive something special for Christmas. She touched the roof of the tiny cupola with its wooden windows painted to resemble stained glass.

"Laurie painted those," Spence said. "We didn't want to use glass."

"You did a beautiful job, Laurie."

The outer walls of the house were a barn red. Unfinished thin gray lines were scrawled across them to represent brick. The roof had been painted black.

"Let me show you this." Rather than turning it around to display four rooms, two up and two down, Spence grabbed miniature knobs on a double door painted on the front and pulled. Wings of the house swung open in both directions, displaying extra rooms at each side and creating eight in all.

Phoebe gasped. "I don't know what to say."

He fidgeted, his voice cautious as he said, "Tell us you like it."

His face swam before her as tears teemed in her eyes. "What amazing work. I was right in thinking you could create something that outshone the one in the store. Thank you." She wrapped Laurie in a hug. "Both of you."

"Hugging my sister hardly seems fair when I did most of the work." Spence teased her with an exaggerated frown.

Phoebe stood on her tiptoes, ready to wrap her arms around him, but his wink and a realization of what she was about to do scorched her skin with the heat of a lightning bolt. An impulsive act, based on excitement, could open a door better left closed.

"Thank you, Spence." She spun on her toes without touching him and grabbed the first piece of wallpaper under her hand. "This will work."

Laurie stared at her. "I thought you said Maura would prefer something brighter."

Phoebe looked at her choice, a patterned gray as dull as anything she had ever seen. "You're right. I meant the blue one and the one with the yellow fruit for the dining room."

Her attempt to laugh off the mistake fell flat.

SPENCE ENTERED HIS office at the same time Phoebe placed an

envelope on his desk. "Here again on an off day?"

She flinched and whipped around. Guilt paraded in the progressive shades of pink coloring her face.

"I had no idea you liked our store so well." He expected the lighthearted remark to put her at ease, but the straight line of her lips said she would have none of it.

She snatched the envelope from the desk and held it out to him. "I wanted to leave this."

He read his name on the front but didn't touch it. "What is it?"

"Payment for the dollhouse."

She thought he intended to sell it to her? "I don't want payment, Phoebe."

"Please take it."

"No." Seeing the glow on her face yesterday was worth every hour spent in his workshop. He wanted no other compensation.

Her stubborn chin rose to attention. "Then I'm afraid I can't accept the dollhouse."

"You're the one who asked me to make it for Maura. Now you won't accept it?"

"I asked to trade, but things are different now. Working here and playing for the Davidsons has provided more than enough to pay you."

He shut the door, stalked to the other side of his desk, and rearranged a group of papers to keep his hand from seizing that envelope and tearing it into tiny pieces. "Keep your money."

Phoebe turned to face him. "You're angry?"

"I'm not angry."

"You sound angry."

"I'm not angry." Maybe a little.

All right, yes, he walked a fine line between anger and disappointment. When she'd backed away from him yesterday as if he were a wolf ready to devour her, that was disappointment. When realizing nothing he'd done had moved them past her qualms over his motivations, that was disappointment. When thinking over his flirtation in the workshop left him with an inclination to kick himself into Sunday, *that* was anger.

"You and Laurie put hours of work into something for a child you barely know, Spence. I won't take advantage of you. What about the materials? I'm sure they cost you."

She was not about to let this go. "I can afford a few pieces of wood. It was something I wanted to do. For Maura."

And for her mother.

Her expression softened. "I appreciate it but would feel better if you took the money."

"I don't want it, Phoebe."

"I won't give my daughter something that costs me nothing. We'll trade."

He fought to control an unexpected urge to laugh at her tenacity. "Haven't we been through this before? What is your offer this time, Mrs. Crain?"

"I'm willing to play for the store through New Year's with no compensation."

Before he could tell her to forget it, someone knocked on his door. "Come in."

"Spence, have you seen Gil today?" Roslyn marched into the office, a paper clenched in her hand. Her red and puffy-eyed glance shifted from him to Phoebe and back. "I'm sorry. You and Mrs. Crain are busy. I'll come back."

Phoebe placed the envelope on the desk. "No. I'll go and let you two talk."

"We're not done...negotiating, Mrs. Crain." Spence pointed to a second chair. "Stay."

She looked to Roslyn, who said, "It's all right. Anything said here will be all over the store shortly anyway."

Phoebe sat in the chair he indicated and turned her head away, as if doing so made her unable to hear whatever he and Roslyn were about to discuss.

Spence leaned against the corner of the desk. "Tell me the problem, Roslyn."

"Has Gil come in this morning?"

"I haven't seen him. Why? What's wrong?"

"He's missing."

Chapter Fourteen

Spence wavered between believing his friend was missing and believing Roslyn exaggerated.

"Gil met with a man at the house last night. They got into an argument and started shouting at one another."

"Who was the man?"

"I've never met him."

"What was the argument about?"

She rolled the paper tighter, then unrolled it and held it out to him. "This, I think."

Spence scanned the form. "Where did you get this?"

"When the man left, Gil was in a foul mood—not unusual these days. We fought, and I drove to the farm to get away from him and calm down."

They must have had quite a quarrel for Roslyn to run off to her parents' farm. According to Gil, she despised being associated with the place.

"I returned a couple of hours later. He'd packed his clothes and gone."

Phoebe shifted on the seat to face Roslyn, her expression hard. "Are you all right?"

"Fine."

"Like you, I'm sure he needed time to calm down. He'll be back." Spence hoped that was the case. Gil owed him some answers about the paper Roslyn had handed him.

"I don't think so. He hadn't returned by this morning, so I went through what remained of his things, looking for something to tell me where he'd gone. The fireplace in the sitting room was cold, but it held the ashes of burned paper."

"Where did you find this?" Spence held up the form.

"On the floor under his desk. I imagine it fell without him realizing it."

Phoebe stretched to see. "What is it?"

Spence's chest tightened as he read and reread the company name—*R. B. Connors and Company, Wholesalers, Peru, Indiana.* "It's a blank invoice form." Though not from one of their main suppliers. He turned it over. Nothing typed or written on either side. "When Gil argued with the other man, what exactly did you hear?"

"Only words here and there. For instance, I heard *discovery* and *bank*"—she bit her lip—"your name, and *police.* That's why I brought that paper here. I'm just a farm girl, but I'm sure something is wrong, something that involves the store. Why would he have another company's blank invoice at home?"

Why indeed? "I'll take care of this, Roslyn. You're upset. Why don't you go home for the day?"

"If you don't mind, working will keep me from dwelling on Gil and whatever happens with this situation."

Spence hesitated. Could he trust her to do her work without letting her concerns get in the way? He nodded. "All right."

Phoebe rose and took Roslyn's arm. "Let's have a cup of tea before you start work." She glanced at Spence. "We'll be on the third floor if you need us."

Once the ladies left, Spence studied the form. Why would Gil possess a blank invoice form from a wholesaler? And what were the other papers he'd burned? More forms?

What are you up to, Gil, and where have you gone?

He strode down the hall, his unease growing with each step. It intensified when seeing his friend's office lit only by the little sunlight able to penetrate the drawn window shade. The desk was neat and vacant, personal items missing. Nothing but the lingering smell of old cigar smoke.

The man Spence had considered a friend had left with no intention of returning.

He asked the clerks in the accounting area if they had handled invoices from the company identified on the paper Roslyn had found. No one admitted to recognizing the name, so he left them with instructions to go through the files seeking anything pertaining to R. B. Connors Wholesalers, then marched to his father's office. Each step weighed him down with guilt and incompetence. He should have contacted the police long ago.

Spence explained Roslyn's visit and Gil's disappearance before he showed his father the form. "Are you familiar with this company?"

"No. Could he have begun his own business?"

"If so, Roslyn knows nothing about it."

"It wouldn't take much to fill out a blank form like that. It could explain the missing merchandise."

Merchandise paid for yet nonexistent.

Spence didn't like that his father's thoughts led in the same direction as his own. *Embezzler* was a nasty title. Doubly so when applied to a friend.

His father tapped the tips of his fingers together as he thought, then he stood and grabbed his coat and hat from the rack in the corner of his office. "Let's go."

"Where are we going?"

"I know he's your friend, but I smell a foul odor that needs airing. It's time to get the police involved."

If their suspicions proved valid, airing that odor was sure to mean scandal, and scandal meant trouble for the store and failure on Spence's part. After all, he had hired Gil.

"I'LL TAKE IT FOR YOU." Phoebe reached for the container that held trash from the women's clothing department.

Claire pulled the box to her chest. "It's not your job."

"No, but will you deny me the opportunity to help you?" Phoebe sounded like Spence when he said he'd built the dollhouse to please Maura.

He'd spent hours laboring over her daughter's gift as she had labored over the scarves for the children. Mr. Jernigan hadn't offered to pay her or her Widow's Might friends. If he had, he would have offended each woman. Was that how Spence had felt when she'd insisted on paying him for the dollhouse? Had she offended him?

He'd kept the money these past two days, so she considered the subject closed but didn't like thinking she had hurt his feelings.

"Has anyone pointed out how mulish you can be?" If Claire didn't already have her hands full, Phoebe could see her flopping them on her hips as she asked the question.

"Too often." Phoebe wiggled her fingers. "Give it here."

Claire handed her the box. "Go with my undying appreciation for your sacrifice."

"I'm not going to war."

"Say that after you've smelled the trash heap." She held her nose.

Phoebe shook her head. "Goodbye, Claire."

She carried the trash to a back door and down the outer stairs to the end of the alley between the store and warehouse building. At the street, a large wooden box held the refuse from the store, most of it anyway. It overflowed because of the city's sporadic pick up and proved Claire right when she said carrying out the trash would be a sacrifice...a sacrifice involving her sense of smell. The sooner she completed her task, the better.

On a brighter note, it was too cold for the flies to congregate.

Too short to place the box on top of the pile, she stood on her toes and shoved it as high as possible, knocking something metal to the ground. Embarrassed, she looked around. The clatter had drawn the attention of two men standing at the corner of the alley across the street.

Phoebe squinted. She didn't recognize the shorter man, but was the other Gil Malone? Everyone assumed he'd left Riverport the night Roslyn had seen him arguing with another man. Phoebe had only seen Roslyn's husband once, and this man wore his hat low. She might be wrong.

Noting her stare, both men turned and disappeared down the alley. Maybe she wasn't wrong about seeing Gil Malone, because men with nothing to hide didn't run away.

And those men ran.

SPENCE SAT IN HIS FATHER'S office with his eyes closed. With one finger, he rubbed the area starting at the bridge of his nose up to his hairline and back down. The kneading did nothing to relieve the headache that had persisted since learning of Gil's embezzlement.

In the seat across from him, an officer from the Riverport Police Department recounted the outcome of their investigation into Gil Malone's disappearance two days ago and the blank invoice Roslyn had found.

"We've inquired into the name on the invoice"—the policeman consulted a small notepad—"this R. B. Connors and Company. As far as we can tell, there's no such business anywhere in the state. We also checked banks within fifty miles of Riverport."

Spence sat up. He hadn't thought about bank accounts. "What did you find?"

With the expansive grin, the officer's teeth showed for the first time under his mustache. "We found an account for the company at a Peru bank. I've sent a man there with the photo we received from Gilbert

Malone's wife. He'll be back tonight and will tell us all we need to know about the account holder and any deposits or withdrawals."

After scouring the account books and files, the clerks had uncovered four invoices from the wholesaler that totaled $165 in merchandise—small amounts that wouldn't attract attention.

None of their records showed any such merchandise sold or in inventory. They were phantom goods that pointed to theft through falsified invoices prepared and approved by Gil. Spence's friend not only stole from the store, he sat across from Spence and lied through his teeth.

The Second asked, "You have no leads on Malone's whereabouts?"

"No, sir. We're making inquiries."

Losing less than two hundred dollars would not ruin the Newlands, but the ashes of the burned papers bothered Spence. Were they all the same forms, or were there other fraudulent companies set up to steal from the store? Companies they still knew nothing about?

Worse, how long would it have gone on if Gil hadn't gotten scared?

IF IT TURNED OUT PHOEBE was wrong about seeing Gil Malone in the alley, so be it, because if she said nothing, she chanced his getting away.

While waiting at the elevator, she brushed from her eyes a lock of hair loosened from its pins. The move revealed Mary Alice Davidson walking toward her, flaunting a cat-that-ate-the-canary smirk.

"Good afternoon, Miss Langford."

"Good afternoon, Miss Davidson. I prefer Mrs. Crain."

"I'm sure you do."

Phoebe tapped her toe on the floor, as though the action would hasten the arrival of the elevator and a quick getaway.

Mary Alice laid a hand on Phoebe's arm. "I should have provided you with my condolences the other night."

Condolences? "I don't know what you're talking about."

"On the loss of your daughter's father, of course."

The loss of her daughter's father? An odd way to state it and one that prickled the flesh on Phoebe's arms. She used the same description for Douglas. "Thank you, but that was a long time ago."

"I've heard one never gets over such a tragedy. For instance, we know of parents in St. Louis who lost a son, a wife her husband, and children their father. Douglas died almost six years ago, and Mr. Alder says his daughter-in-law, my friend Helen, has never gotten over her husband's death."

Phoebe locked her knees to keep from collapsing. She didn't dare look away, even though the satisfaction in Mary Alice's expression affirmed her pleasure over having hit her mark. Jealousy truly had warped the woman's mind.

"Does Spence know your daughter is a—"

"Don't say it!" Phoebe's shout used up the rest of the oxygen in her lungs. She drew in a deep and shuddering breath.

Mary Alice stepped closer. "Did you really think Helen Alder didn't know about you and her husband?"

The elevator door opened and Spence stepped out. His arched brows and stiff posture confirmed that he had heard. Everything.

Phoebe's muscles ached with the effort to remain where she stood and not run away. She had done more than enough running over the years. It was time to face her past.

Chapter Fifteen

"Hello, Spence."

He ignored Mary Alice and studied Phoebe. The way she stood hunched and partially turned away added credence to what he'd overheard while descending in the cage—to what a number of Newland's customers had probably heard.

First, he'd been wrong about Gil. Now he learned Phoebe had a disreputable past. The headache raged on.

Mary Alice batted sympathetic eyelids at him. "I'm so sorry you heard that, Spence."

Right.

"I should go." Her task complete, she escaped the devastation she'd wrought.

Three women paused on the nearby staircase to take in the show. Spence grasped Phoebe's arm and dragged her toward the back of the store and away from gawkers—witnesses to her shame. He'd expected a fight from her but didn't get one.

Once they were outside, he led her at a slower pace down the street and toward the river. Neither of them said a word as they paused on the bank and watched water flow past a thin layer of ice along the edge.

A train whistle wailed. The sound enhanced the fire in his head but brought Maura to mind. What that child would face through the fiendish actions of her parents and Mary Alice!

"Why a train?"

"What?"

"Why would you tell your daughter a father would arrive on a train?"

In a voice barely audible, she said, "Maura asked over and over about where fathers came from. I grew impatient with her questions and told her trains were where princes and princesses met. It was the first thing that occurred to me, because it's how I met her father. It sounds silly, but..."

"I suppose you think it was a happy memory." How could a relationship with a married man be happy? It went against everything Spence believed in.

"There is little happiness in that memory. I wish I had never boarded that train. I wish I'd never met Douglas." She covered her face and her shoulders heaved several times, as though she tried to contain her emotions. Then she dropped her arms to her sides. "That isn't true. If I had never met him, I wouldn't have Maura, and she's the joy of my life."

Spence had walked out of the store without an overcoat, and the cold penetrated his suit. As much as he wanted to go back inside, he wanted more to hear her account of what had happened. He wanted to believe he hadn't been as wrong about her as he had Gil.

"It won't be long before Mary Alice's story will be common knowledge, and your daughter will suffer. What will you tell her?"

Phoebe glared at him. "Don't you really want me to tell you Mary Alice lied?"

"I know she didn't lie. I saw it on your face." He fought to control his frustration. "I'm concerned about Maura. What will you tell her about her father?"

"I will tell her the truth." Her gaze bore into him. "I was never married to Douglas."

Her eyes expanded like a fist opening after it punched him in the gut.

Spence knew it was coming, pushed her into admitting it, but yes, he had wished he was mistaken in what he'd heard or that Mary Alice had lied.

Apparently not.

PHOEBE HAD LONGED TO keep her sin—though unintentional—forever between herself, her mother, and God.

She waited for Spence's condemnation, but he only stared at her. She whispered, "Don't look at me that way."

He turned his head and watched the river again, his profile bold, chin strong. "What you said... It caught me by surprise."

Phoebe set her jaw. She had asked forgiveness for her part. Why should she continue to go through life ashamed when her fault was in trusting that a man had integrity? Why should she let Spence think the worst of her without explanation?

"When I was seventeen, I traveled by train for a performance. With few unoccupied seats in the car, Douglas asked to sit next me. We talked the entire trip." Despite the desire to remain detached from the memories of a first love, her voice drifted into a mellow, wistful tone. "He was charming, funny, handsome. We continued to see one another, and after two months, we said our vows before a judge."

"But you said..."

"He tricked me into believing we were married."

A low moan escaped Spence's throat.

"We moved into a comfortable house a few miles outside of St. Louis. Even though he was gone quite often, I was a happy bride. The day I learned about Maura, I couldn't wait to tell him." Phoebe wiped hot tears from her eyes with the heel of her hand. "He was furious and called me names I never dreamed a man would say to me. That's when he told me we weren't legally married. 'How can we be,' he said, 'when I'm already married?'"

She waited for Spence to say something. Anything. When he

didn't, she swallowed as if a block of ice had lodged in her throat. "After he stomped out the door, I didn't know what to do, so I followed him into the city. That's when I learned he spoke the truth. I saw his wife. I saw two small children."

Spence still stood rigid, not responding. Could he not accept her innocence? Could he not see the pain she had experienced?

"I was young and thought he was the sun, moon, and stars rolled up in one glorious person." Then the clouds rolled in and obscured her view of romantic love. "In my inexperience with men, I made the biggest mistake of my life."

He turned cold eyes on her. Gone was the smile she'd become accustomed to seeing. "After the way he treated you, you continue to call yourself Mrs. Crain."

She rubbed her arms. "Crain was the name on our marriage certificate—as false as everything else. What was I supposed to do to protect my child?"

"You never confronted him? Publicly shamed him?"

"And forever brand my daughter with a contemptible label?"

With that, he lost the hostility and hung his head. "You're right. Maura doesn't deserve the shame."

And she did?

"Is he really dead?"

Phoebe nodded. "A riding accident three weeks before Maura was born. I read it in the newspaper."

He stood in silence for a moment before asking, "Why didn't you return to performing?"

"I did the other night, remember? Look what happened." She scoffed at her foolishness in thinking she could go back to her career. "I've scraped by all this time terrified of someone discovering the truth. Because I thought I could resume my old life, my daughter will suffer. My mother will suffer."

Spence had called her as frosty as a windowpane, and with good reason. She felt no less frosty now. "How could someone like you understand what it's like to lose everything to a young man with the resources and willingness to break a woman's heart as a prank? Douglas wasn't the only one of his friends who found it amusing to turn a woman's world upside down and inside out. It was a game they played."

Spence stepped back as if she had slapped him. "That's why you were cold toward me. Even after these past weeks, you saw no difference in us?"

"Douglas treated me like a princess...until he'd finished with me."

"One of the things drummed into me from an early age is that all women are worthy of respect and courteous treatment. I've taken that teaching to heart. I am *nothing*"—his hand cut through the air—"like the man who deceived you."

Long, powerful strides carried him away.

Phoebe remained at the river, December's cold chilling the dampness on her face. Visions of all Spence had done for her rolled through her mind: driving her to the orphanage, building the dollhouse, providing her with a job, speaking with sensitivity to Maura. Douglas wouldn't have hesitated to do those things if he thought it was to his advantage.

What made Spencer Newland the Third different?

Somehow, he had broken through her barrier of distrust. Somehow, he *was* different. She believed it, yet she couldn't find the voice to assure him of her change of heart until he was gone.

"I know you're nothing like Douglas." The whispered response drifted away on the water's current.

Chapter Sixteen

S pence rubbed the ache in his forehead and dropped the newspaper onto his desk. "There will be no new stores."

His father sat in the chair across from Spence's desk, one leg over the other, his calm expression a contrast to Spence's inner turmoil. "Whether or not Mrs. Crain actually saw Malone, the police know he opened the bank account in Peru. They'll track him down, along with his partner."

"That means an arrest, a trial, and more notoriety. It was bad enough to read of the embezzlement this morning."

"You're making too much of this."

"Father, I haven't given up on Clifton Lark, but if the Chicago papers pick up this story, what chance do we have at a partnership with him or anyone else?"

"Spence—"

"Between Gil and Phoebe, I've made mistakes and endangered the reputation of Newland's. How can you trust me not to lose everything you and Grandfather worked so hard to attain?" He muttered, "All this does is prove Grandfather right."

His father's graying eyebrows punctuated his bewilderment. "Prove him right about what?"

Spence had gone a dozen years keeping the frustration to himself and shouldn't have said anything. Then again, it might be time to get it out in the open. "Years ago, I overheard him talking to you about my future. He said you should find someone else to run our businesses. He doubted I'd be strong enough."

What if his sister married Pittman? Spence liked Wallace but couldn't see the young man in charge of Newland's interests.

His father sat deep in thought before his shoulders surged with a drawn-out sigh. "It's true that the long-term future of our assets concerned my father, but the danger to you worried him more. He was afraid the responsibility would put an additional strain on your health as an adult.

"What you overheard was a suggestion that we prepare for the *possibility* of a day when someone outside the family would have control. Later, he regretted reacting on emotion, and the idea that you might never be at the helm broke his heart."

Spence couldn't count how often, as a lonely child lying in bed with a fever, headache, or other malady, his family had prayed over his health. He shut his eyes and conjured scene after scene. One man occupied those images more than anyone else—the man who entertained him, prayed with him and for him, laughed with him.

"Son, he often talked about your intelligence, your intuitiveness, and your compassion for the suffering of others. He found those to be gifts far more commendable than your ability to run a business. I wish he had lived to see the strong and dependable man you've become."

It was though his grandfather's voice broke through a wad of cotton stuffing Spence's ears. Had he overreacted all these years? Had his young mind blown up the little bit he'd heard and let it govern his present thoughts and actions?

Spence leaned back in his chair, seeing his grandfather sitting in his room, joking and praying, cheering up a miserable little boy. Why had he allowed his mind to take one memory as truth and distort the rest? How had he come to resent the man as much as he loved him? "I should have known better. I spent years believing we'd let each other down on the basis of one overheard fragment of conversation."

"You have never been a disappointment to any of us."

A slight smile brightened Spence's dreary deliberations...for a few seconds. "None of what's been said changes the fact that I've made mistakes that could cost us dearly."

His father frowned. "Is this still about Gil Malone, or does it have more to do with Mrs. Crain?"

"Both, I suppose. Do you think Lark will want to have his name associated with two scandals?"

"You told me Mrs. Crain wasn't at fault. That she'd been duped into thinking her marriage was real. I thought you accepted her story."

"I did. For what that man did to Phoebe and Maura, if he weren't dead already, Father, I'd be tempted to pummel him until he wished he were."

"It sounds as if there's more to your feelings in the matter than anxiety over the store. For what it's worth, our receipts are up by eight percent on the days she's here. I'd like to see her continue to play on a regular basis."

"That was before Mary Alice slashed her reputation. Aren't you afraid of the impact of Phoebe's story on our customers?"

His father leaned forward in his seat. "What's really bothering you?"

Spence ran the palm of his hand down his mustache. The bristly stubble under his fingertips reminded him he hadn't shaved this morning and of how little sleep he'd gotten after what happened with Phoebe. "She should have told me."

"Put yourself in her place, son. Why would she tell you her deepest and darkest secret? You're not courting. You're not engaged."

"I've tried to be her friend, but she sees me as another spoiled son of a wealthy man. As far she's concerned, I'm not someone to be trusted with her emotions." He sank back in the chair and mumbled, "Lately, nothing has gone as I've planned it."

"Listen to yourself. *Your* plans. *Your* efforts. *Your* failure. If you were to ask me, Spence, there's been a greater miscommunication in your life than getting the wrong impression from your grandfather's words." The Second rose from his seat and paused at the door. "The First wasn't any more perfect than you or the rest of us, but do you remember what he said kept him humble, kept him going? Whenever he felt as though everything good in his life had resulted from his own efforts, he would read Second Corinthians twelve."

How well Spence remembered hearing that chapter from his grandfather.

"When was the last time *you* read those verses?"

The Second walked out of the office, leaving Spence alone with his shame. First, not entrusting his efforts to the Lord's will for his life and his family's future.

Then there was Phoebe.

Why would she tell you her deepest and darkest secret?

He saw himself marching away from her at the river. When she did tell him her secret, his feelings had been all that mattered. Where was the sympathy and compassion his grandfather had seen in him? The understanding?

I'll never let you fall.

What a liar he turned out to be.

The pounding in his head grew stronger and steadier. Not only had he let her fall, he had tossed her aside. He had broken her trust.

He'd acted in as spoiled and untrustworthy a manner as she'd expected to receive from him, thinking only of his hurt feelings and his family's reputation.

Douglas Alder had nothing on Spencer Fanning Newland the Third.

He locked his office door, then reached into the drawer of his desk, pulled out the Bible he kept there, and turned to the chapter his grandfather had referenced over and over. He paid special attention to the words that spoke loudest to him.

"And lest I should be exalted above measure through the

abundance of the revelations, there was given to me a thorn in the flesh, the messenger of Satan to buffet me, lest I should be exalted above measure."

Lest Spence should exalt himself.

For years he had let an emotional wound fester until he relied on his own efforts and his own ideas to prove his grandfather wrong. Rather than relying on God, he had put his trust in exercise, diet, and determination. Yes, he'd gained physical strength, but he still suffered from headaches. His thorn in the flesh?

"Therefore, I take pleasure in infirmities, in reproaches, in necessities, in persecutions, in distresses for Christ's sake: for when I am weak, then am I strong."

He had never considered his infirmities in a positive light or used them to glorify Christ. How could he call himself healthy—strong—when his faith in his Lord and others proved weaker than his body when at its frailest moment?

"My grace is sufficient for thee: for my strength is made perfect in weakness. Most gladly therefore will I rather glory in my infirmities, that the power of Christ may rest upon me."

Spence read the entire chapter three times and confessed his foolish actions, his lack of faith and compassion, and his self-centeredness and vanity in thinking he knew best. He truly was a weak man.

Be my strength, Lord, and never let me exalt myself over You.

Perhaps he couldn't admit to taking "pleasure in infirmities," but discovering the truth about himself might make them more bearable.

PHOEBE STOOD AT THE back door of S. F. Newland's and Company, paying little heed to the tiny flakes of snow that drifted onto her head and shoulders. Every inch of her wanted to spin around and run back home.

She had hoped to hear that Spence forgave her and could overlook her past to preserve what had become a growing friendship between them. The silence in the last two days disconcerted her.

The longer she'd lingered at the river after he'd left, the harder she had cried out to be delivered of the bitterness she'd harbored in her heart since learning of Douglas's hoax.

Over the years, she had transferred that bitterness to other men she deemed in a position to do something similar to her or another woman. In getting to know Spence, God had shown her the error in her thinking. She had no right to permit her fear and prejudice to cause her to crush the innocent as she once was crushed.

Instead of God turning a deaf ear to her pleas, she had turned a deaf ear to Him and His desire that she see how she'd shriveled into a sour and cynical harpy when in the company of certain people.

Phoebe turned the knob and entered the building. For the past two days, she had waited for word of her dismissal. Without an official notification of termination, staying home would only add fuel to the rumors. However, stepping into the building opened her up to ridicule and speculation from the other employees and, no doubt, customers. It was the type of humiliation she had tried to avoid for five years.

She rode the elevator to the fourth floor, deposited her coat and hat in the salon, then rode in the cage back to the first floor. During both trips, the elevator operator, always courteous in the past, avoided conversation and eye contact with her. She considered it an overture to the rest of her day.

As Phoebe crossed the floor, Claire and Roslyn met her halfway to the piano. Most of her Widow's Might friends had visited her home to express their concern and encouragement. Though they never asked for details, she couldn't bear to have them think poorly of her and had provided her side of the story. Without those friendships and their prayers, she might still be lying in bed feeling sorry for herself.

Claire wrapped her in a hug right in the middle of the store. "I'm glad you haven't let Miss Davidson scare you away."

The show of support settled Phoebe's nerves like nothing else. "Not yet."

Roslyn's firm grip added additional comfort. "If anyone gives you trouble, let me know." She winked. "We outcasts need to stick together."

"You're no outcast, Roslyn. What happened wasn't your fault."

"It was. More than you know. I can say I didn't steal the store's money. I can't say I didn't drive Gil to it." Roslyn sighed. "We never belonged together."

With the revelation by Mary Alice, Phoebe hadn't told Spence about possibly seeing Gil Malone. Instead, she'd told Claire, who'd passed the information on. The police had searched, but they had found no clues to the man's whereabouts.

"Thank you. Both of you." She swiped at the moisture that leaked from her eyes.

Roslyn pulled out a handkerchief and handed it to her. "I owe you one."

Phoebe glanced toward the front of the store where the piano waited for her...if Spence hadn't moved it back to his house.

"It's still there, and we'll be listening." Claire patted Phoebe's shoulder, then climbed the stairs to her station on the third floor.

Like ants crawling up the back of her neck, the stares of various clerks and a few customers followed her to the piano.

She sat on the small bench, her heart pinching a little at not seeing Spence along the way.

God, I know you are listening. I believe this is what you want of me. Give me the courage to do it.

Deliberately chosen, cheerful melodies lifted her mood. Once in a while, a store customer stopped to listen to her play. Some walked by with their noses in the air. Others seemed oblivious to her presence.

Near the end of her two hours, Laurie Newland approached the piano and stood in the curve, as her brother had done so often. "Good morning, Phoebe. I'm glad to see you here. We weren't sure you would come."

"I have a responsibility." Phoebe continued to play "Silent Night."

Leaning forward and in a voice that commanded attention, Laurie said, "Please stop playing. I have something important to tell you. Spence's office is empty. We can talk in private."

Phoebe rested her hands in her lap. Why would the Newland's send the youngest member of the family to fire her? Was Spence still so incensed he couldn't bring himself to be near her? What about his father?

Once they reached the office, Laurie closed the door and gestured for Phoebe to sit in one of the chairs near the desk. She angled a second chair to face Phoebe. "I don't know the details of what happened between you and Spence, but he's had a rough few days, spending most of the time in his room with a migraine."

Phoebe's shoulders sank. Had she caused his suffering? "I'm sorry. I never meant—"

"Don't be sorry. He said it's given him time to think and pray. Actually, I think it was good for him."

Phoebe marveled at the girl's impassioned viewpoint. "You told him that?"

Laurie waved a hand through the air. "Yes, but don't think me heartless. He agreed, and he feels much better."

Not wanting to be caught in his office should he return, Phoebe said, "You wanted to talk to me?"

"Spence received a telegram from Mr. Lark, requesting a visit."

"That's good news, isn't it? I know how hard Spence has tried to gain his support."

"There were no promises, but my brother told me he believes God opened this door and expects him to walk through it. Before he left, he arranged for Maura's gift to be delivered to your house."

At least she had accomplished one thing. Maura would have a good

Christmas. But even that was Spence's doing.

Laurie placed her hand over Phoebe's. "Don't be angry with him."

"I'm not."

Phoebe was angry at herself for her treatment of him.

Chapter Seventeen

The hack pulled up in front of a mansion on Prairie Avenue, and Spence peered out the window at the Romanesque architectural style of Clifton Lark's house. Although Spence's parents owned one of the largest and finest homes in Riverport, the corner towers and red stone facade of the Lark house outshone it from the basement up.

With its prime location near downtown and the lakeshore, many of Chicago's wealthy called the Prairie Avenue area home, evidenced by the structures he'd passed along the way. Down the street sat the mansion belonging to Marshall Field. While he was in the city, he planned to visit the man's store—a scouting mission of sorts.

The dregs of a headache still lingered, but try as hard as it might, the pain couldn't conquer his exhilaration. He left the hack, opened the wrought iron gate, and sauntered up the wide steps to the front door as if he belonged. According to the telegram in his pocket, he did.

A moment after Spence rang the bell, he was ushered inside by a butler who took his coat and hat, then led him to a sitting room with a roaring fire to sip coffee and wait for his host.

What a whirlwind few days. Due to Lark's telegram being misplaced by a telegraph clerk, Spence had a mere two hours to prepare in order to catch the train that would get him here in time for his appointment. He'd thrown a few clothes into a valise, along with a copy of the proposal he'd given Mrs. Lark when she'd visited Riverport.

The whole time, Spence asked God to block his travel if the trip wasn't in His plan.

On the train, he'd prayed for direction in dealing with Clifton Lark. If the door to a partnership between them shut, he trusted God had a better plan. For the first time, he left the situation in His hands.

Lark's summons had come at an inconvenient time in his personal life. Would Phoebe forgive him for walking away from her at the river? For acting like that spoiled, self-centered man she had believed him to be? He hoped the letter of apology he'd written her would suffice until he saw her on Christmas Eve.

Juliet Lark entered the room, and Spence bolted to his feet. She was young—about thirty-five—intelligent, mature, and thoroughly familiar with her husband's business.

"I'm sorry to keep you waiting, Mr. Newland. Clifton is eager to meet you."

"May I ask what changed his mind about seeing me?"

"I'll let him explain."

Mrs. Lark led him to a room on the first floor, where a secretary sat behind a desk. The man nodded, then continued typing as she opened the door behind him.

They entered an office with rich paneled walls. Dark curtains were drawn across the windows, and electric lights took the place of the sun to light the interior. A man about Spence's father's age sat at a round table to the right, opposite a large desk and bookshelves. When he saw them, he stood but remained in place.

"Thank you for coming, Mr. Newland." Dressed in a fine suit, and with thinning gray hair and a salt-and-pepper beard trimmed and neat, Clifton Lark resembled any other businessman of Spence's acquaintance—with one exception. Haunted eyes darted to the door that his wife had shut with haste after she entered the room.

Lark blinked away whatever troubled him and gestured to the familiar object on the table. "I want to thank you for the cigar box."

The gift had begun as a well-meaning bribe, but today Spence could truly say it was his pleasure to make it for the man. "You're welcome, sir."

"Please have a seat."

Spence joined him at the table.

"You and your family impressed Juliet during her visit last month. She told me Newland's department store and its owners met all her expectations."

"Thank you, Mrs. Lark."

Even with the lighting from various lamps and wall sconces, Spence longed to pull back the heavy curtains and expose the room and everything in it to the sunlight.

"I'm sure you've wondered why I sent my wife last month and didn't come myself," Lark said.

"To be honest, yes, sir."

Lark glanced at his wife, who nodded. "The truth is that, for the past year, I've rarely left this house."

In Spence's experience, there was only one reason a person would be confined to his home. "You're ill?"

"In a manner of speaking. Are you familiar with agoraphobia?"

"Agora..."

Mrs. Lark pulled up a chair next to her husband and placed her hand in his. "It's a mental condition, Mr. Newland. Several months ago, the doctors diagnosed Clifton as suffering from it."

A mental condition? Had he tried to enlist the aid of a lunatic?

"There's nothing to be afraid of. Agoraphobia causes a terror of certain locations or situations. It keeps the patient from leaving a particular space or circumstance in which they feel safe. In my husband's case, it's this house."

"I didn't know."

"Few people do. We try to protect him from those who wouldn't understand."

For some reason, they had decided he would. He turned to her husband. "Why tell me?"

"Your gift and Juliet's report intrigued me, so I made inquiries into you and your family. From it, I learned of your childhood difficulties."

Spence bristled. His past wasn't a secret, but he'd worked hard to prove...

No need to stroll that path again.

"You know what it's like to want to take part in the world and be unable to do so."

"Yes, sir. I do."

"I hope you can also understand that my condition is something I prefer to keep from the public."

Not only would it open up Mr. Lark's character to ridicule, but news such as this could have a detrimental effect on his finances. "No one will hear it from me."

The man opened the cigar box. "I realize your goal was to attract my attention with this, Mr. Newland, but you have a gift—a God-given one."

Spence was realizing all the gifts lavished on him during his lifetime. A close family. The joy of music. Financial advantages. The strengthening of his body. Most importantly, the gift that would endure throughout all eternity. An everlasting gift of hope given by the One whose birth they prepared to celebrate.

Perhaps soon he would count two more—a woman whose frost had begun to melt and a little girl with a sunshine smile.

They spoke of one topic after another, none of them involving the financing of five-and-ten-cent stores. The man's intelligence and sense of humor shone through the conversation, undamaged by his illness.

The clock on the wall chimed.

"Mr. Newland, I apologize for monopolizing the conversation for over two hours."

When Clifton Lark rose, Spence interpreted it as a signal to leave, and rose also. "Not at all. This has been a pleasure. Thank you for inviting me."

Mrs. Lark asked, "Won't you stay for supper?"

"If you'll forgive me, tomorrow is Christmas Eve. I'd like to be in Riverport."

"Of course. You want to be home with your family."

And others. "Yes, ma'am."

"Thank you for coming. It isn't often I interact with strangers these days. Learning about what you went through as a child and have accomplished as a man has given me a more optimistic outlook." Mr. Lark walked with him toward the door and stopped a few feet away. "About your new stores—your proposal makes it difficult to say no, but until I can defeat this fear and see to my mental fitness, my doctors have advised that I not undertake any additional burdens."

"I understand." Spence shook the man's hand. He turned to go, then stopped and faced his host. "Sir, I urge you to not make my mistake and take your healing onto yourself. I've only begun to understand that God works for His glory even in our weaknesses."

Lark responded with a slow smile. "I do have something for you before you leave." He pulled a sheet of paper from his waistcoat pocket. "This is the name and address of a close friend who lives down the street. He's a good man, trustworthy and generous. I took the liberty of discussing with him your plan for the five-and-ten-cent stores. He's interested in talking with you at his office this afternoon. I would suggest you see him before you return to Riverport."

Spence stared at the sheet of paper Lark held out. His eyes widened at reading the name. The friend was no insignificant businessman.

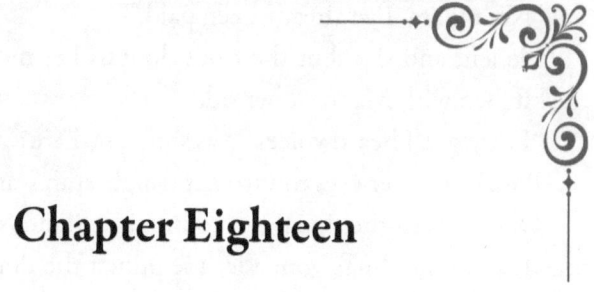

Chapter Eighteen

The stranger on Phoebe's porch held a large wooden box. "Mrs. Crain? I'm Eugene Henry. Mr. Newland sent me."

The dollhouse. Phoebe stared at the box. It was the only thing she'd thought she would ever want from Spence, because it would make Maura happy. After only a month, she wanted much more from him. She wanted her own chance at happiness.

"Please bring it in, but quietly. My daughter is helping her grandmother in the kitchen, and I don't want to attract her attention." She led the way to her mother's bedroom. Hopefully, Maura wouldn't find it there. "You can leave it in that corner."

He placed the box on the floor. "Is this where you want the other one?"

"Other one? I'm not expecting anything else."

"I have a second box on the wagon."

Surely she wasn't being faced with a repetition of the cigar box and its mistaken delivery. "Whose name is on it?"

"Yours, ma'am, and your address. It's also from Newland's."

Why would Spence send anything more than the dollhouse he'd committed to making for Maura, especially after she'd hurt his feelings at the river? "Yes, please bring it in here."

She waited in the room while Mr. Henry went after the second box. When he returned, he carried a crate almost as large as the first one and set it on the floor.

"Let me get you—"

"No, ma'am. I've already been paid."

He left, and she shut the front door as her mother walked out of the kitchen with Maura at her side.

"I thought I heard voices. Was someone here?"

Phoebe cut her eyes toward her daughter in warning.

Oblivious to the signal not to inquire, Maura said, "We're making bread, and Grandma's gonna let me punch the dough." She fisted her little hands and punched the air.

Phoebe ran a hand over her daughter's head. "Don't hurt it."

Maura cocked her head. "Can we go to see the trains?"

"Honey—"

"Pleeease, Mama. Sarah said the people at the station give children a candy cane on Christmas Eve."

Phoebe sighed. What did it matter that they had no tree to hang it from? "After you and Grandma finish the bread, we'll go to the station for a few minutes, but this will be the last time."

Maura ran back to the kitchen. Her grandmother grinned and followed at a more sedate pace.

Phoebe returned to her mother's room and closed the door. She removed the lid of the box she assumed held the dollhouse and dug through the packing material. Thankful the gift arrived in one piece, she fixed her interest on the second mysterious box with her name on the front.

It was about the same height and width as the first one. What did it hold? She glanced at the dollhouse. Of course. What was a child's dollhouse without tiny pieces of furniture? She'd bought a miniature rattan sofa and chairs at Newland's as a start and planned to add to the collection as she could afford it. But it would be like Spence to supply her daughter with a house full of furniture.

Phoebe pulled the cover off and set it aside. On top of the packing material was an envelope—the same envelope she had left on Spence's desk with the payment for the dollhouse. His name had been scratched out and hers written above it. She thought she had settled the issue with him. Evidently, he didn't agree.

The old fear reared its head and warned her against the consequences of expecting something for nothing. She chased it away and opened the envelope. It contained no money, only a sheet of paper, which she unfolded.

Dear Phoebe,

I regret many things these past days, not the least of which is how I walked away from you. Please forgive me for being another man who thought only of himself and caused you pain in the process.

Phoebe's throat clogged. He was apologizing to her?

In my conceit, I found no reason why you could not see past my financial and social circumstances to the man who honors and esteems you in a way he esteems no other woman. Therefore, my actions proved your fears were valid. I beg you, do not let my vanity shatter the prospects for a closer bond between us.

Never.

If it helps, I should have listened to your advice on the day our carriage bogged down in the ditch. I should have depended on God, not only in my pursuit of an investor but in everything. I assure you I am learning to do so and to act on that direction—a lesson that is a long time in coming.

It is my most ardent desire that you will accept a personal apology from me when I return to Riverport on Christmas Eve.

Yours,

Spence

How could she not accept his apology when she owed him one?

P.S. I am keeping the payment for the dollhouse. No, I do not want it, but I have realized the gift is yours to give your daughter, and not mine. The second gift delivered by Mr. Henry is a different matter. It is from me to you.

A gift for her?

Phoebe dug through the second box, tossing aside straw and

strewing it across her mother's floor until she felt flat, satiny wood under her fingers. She pulled out a heavy cabinet stained a rich mahogany color and with four ball feet.

Not large enough to stand on the floor, it was perfect for a table. She opened the double doors on the front, counted ten rows of drawers two inches high, and realized the exact location he meant it to occupy. This was one of the finest sheet music cabinets she had ever seen.

Phoebe batted away the line of tears that careened down her face. Douglas had given her jewelry, flowers, candy, tickets to plays she'd never heard of. Nothing so special as this. Nothing so...her.

She pressed her hands to her head. Christmas Eve. Spence returned today. When? She reread the line in the letter, but it held no clue to the actual arrival time of the train.

Phoebe cleaned up her mother's room and rushed into the kitchen to grab her coat. "I'll be right back."

Before Mama had time to voice the question carved on her face, Phoebe ran out the door and all the way to the train station.

Inside the building, she scurried up to the ticket window. "What time does the train from Chicago arrive?"

He checked his schedule. "Two ten."

A glance at the large clock on the wall told her it was eleven thirty. That gave her time for a quick stop at Newland's before returning home to prepare her gift for Spence.

At almost two o'clock, bundled in coats, hats, and gloves to ward off late December's cold, the three of them left the smell of fresh-baked bread behind and walked to the train station. Phoebe carried a paper-wrapped package and yearned to rush her mother and daughter along, but they had time.

At the station, smoke from a recently arrived train filled the air. Children stood in a long line near the building as they waited to receive a hooked stick of white candy. Parents either stood with them or in groups, talking to friends.

Phoebe balked. Crowds meant a greater chance of someone saying something cruel to her or Maura. Nonetheless, they couldn't live secluded from others, and Phoebe had tired of running. "If you want candy, you'd better get in line."

Maura hung back, her attention on the train. She gasped and tugged on Phoebe's hand to turn her around. "It's him! I knew it would be him. Let's go, Mama."

Phoebe drew an unsteady breath. He was early. She followed Maura, butterfly wings beating inside her stomach.

SPENCE STEPPED OFF the train, ready to inform his parents of his trip, without revealing Clifton Lark's secret. Even though Lark's friend had not agreed to a partnership, the man showed a strong interest, and they would talk again.

God provided. Not Lark and not Spence.

He stretched his shoulders. The movement exposed the tightness in his muscles after sitting on the train for hours.

"It's him! I knew it would be him. Let's go, Mama." Maura's voice rose over the engine's steam and the noise from the other passengers.

Before his delight overpowered him, Spence glanced around to be certain the child's excitement wasn't meant for another man.

Phoebe's gaze latched on to his. She smiled, her stride toward him confident. His own pace quickened until they met in the middle of the station yard. His arms stiffened at his sides to keep from reaching out and pulling her toward him, from enfolding her in his arms and never letting her go.

Not here. But soon.

Maura wrapped her arms around Spence's legs, and he picked her up. "Merry Christmas, Miss Maura."

"Merry Christmas." Her little arms encircled his neck and nearly choked him, but he would never complain.

"Merry Christmas, Phoebe." About to jump out of his skin, he couldn't go another minute without making things right between them. "I'm sorry for the way I responded to you. I promised to never let you fall, and I broke that promise."

"Did you fall, Mama?"

"No, Miss Maura. It was…" How did he explain a mature subject to a five-year-old?

"It was Mr. Newland's way of saying he wants to be friends, darling." She peered up at him with an expression of trust and expectation. His insides lit with the warmth of her smile.

"That's right." It was too early to say he wanted something deeper and grander for them. He and Phoebe needed time to explore the extent of their feelings for one another. Her being here told him the time was coming.

Mrs. White reached for her granddaughter with misshapen fingers. "I'll take her, Mr. Newland. While you and Phoebe talk, we'll be in line for a candy cane."

Standing alone with Phoebe, he restrained the tip of his shoe from toeing the ground like a girl-shy teen. A porter placed his suitcase beside him and left with an ample tip.

Spence led Phoebe to a bench near the building and sat beside her. "I spent the entire train ride going over what I would say to you, how I would apologize in person for my actions."

"You've already explained everything. And the cabinet…" Phoebe breathed a sigh. "It's beautiful, Spence. I'll treasure it."

"Then you read my letter?"

She glanced around, then scooted a little closer. "Would you like to hear my reply?"

"You wrote one?"

"No. But if I had, this is what it would say." She pulled his letter from her purse and unfolded it, then turned it to the blank side and pretended to read. "My dear Spence, I also have regrets, one being that I implied you were no better than Douglas. On the contrary, your integrity and strength of character far exceeds any he could have summoned on his best day.

"What happened at the river was as much my fault as yours. Like you, God has taught me a lesson, and the learning of it was long overdue. Rather than look on the heart as He does, for years I listened to my predetermined judgments and hurt a man I've come to respect and esteem as I have no other." She looked up, regret shining in her eyes. "Given the revelation of my past, it won't be easy, but please do not let gossip and my ignorance destroy your desire for a closer bond between us."

"Oddly enough, I can't remember what you're talking about."

Phoebe laughed, then focused on the paper again. "P.S. This is my Christmas gift to you." She handed him the package she'd been holding. "Merry Christmas."

Spence untied the string and tore off the plain wrapping to reveal a new music book. He flipped through the pages of preprinted staffs, many of them hand-inked with musical notes. His jaw dropped a little more with each new title he read. "These are compositions you've written?"

"Over the years."

His ability to read notes gave him an idea of how the first arrangement in the book might sound. As much as he wanted to search out a piano to play the piece, he tried to give the book back to her. "This is remarkable, Phoebe, but I can't take it. It's too valuable."

She pushed it back at him. "You're right. It is valuable to me, and I want you to have it. Perhaps, in the future, I'll add to it."

He could barely breathe, much less thank her, so he simply took her hand.

"Mama, I got it!" Maura ran up to them with a stick of candy shaped like a shepherd's hook.

At seeing the book on Spence's lap and the discarded paper, Mrs.

White glanced from one to the other of them. A smile formed. "Are we finished here?"

Not yet ready to leave them, he said, "I'll walk the three of you home."

As they left the station, Maura wriggled between Spence and Phoebe. She grabbed the hand of each of them and said, "I told you, Mama. I told you he'd come for Christmas."

Spence stood taller. There was nothing more charming than being the prince in a little girl's fairy tale.

Author Note

Some books almost write themselves. The story and the characters come to mind with little difficulty. Words seem to pour onto the page in the right order. There's a kinship a writer feels with every part of the creation. You were meant to be together!

Unwrapping Hope was not one of those books.

It started with no trouble. I set out to write a Christmas novella, and the idea for the Widow's Might series was born. A book title came to me and, when I saw a certain photo online, so did little Maura and her desire. I envisioned Phoebe receiving a gift by mistake, and her backstory popped out. All that was easy.

Things proved more difficult with Spence. Oh, that man gave me a merry chase. I couldn't pin down his story. I wanted him to go one way, and he wanted to go another. Finally, after a lot of prayer, we met in the middle where all good compromises lie.

I think *Unwrapping Hope* came together well in the end. Look for *Enduring Dreams* in 2020, the first novel in the Widow's Might series. Will Claire Kingsley finally realize her dream?

To keep more of my historical romances coming, I could use your help with any of the following simple, but critical, activities:

Leave an online review with a retailer who sells the book and/or on Goodreads. Your recommendation is important to potential readers. A sentence or two of your honest opinion on the book's retailer page is all it takes.

Tell your reading friends about the book—in-person or online. A word from you can go a long way in convincing others to read it.

Don't miss receiving upcoming releases and special offers. Sign up for the Love and Faith in Fiction newsletter. I'd love having you in the community!

Thanks for your support and for reading my books.

Sandra Ardoin

Acknowledgments

I learn quite a bit with each book I write. Believe me, God uses the spiritual themes of my stories to teach me something. I always pray that they give you, the reader, the same experience. So my first thank you goes to God, who listens to my prayers and yours and guides my steps...and yours.

Next come the people He scatters along the path to publication.

Friend and author Heidi Chiavaroli helped me see that Phoebe's actions in the beginning of the book needed a little tweaking for her to be someone you would like to cheer on. Many thanks for having my back.

My beta buds gave me feedback on the story as a whole to help me bring you the best possible entertainment. I'm so thankful for the insights from Edwina Cowgill, Gail Johnson, Judy Welbaum, and Glenda Wilhelm. You came through for me, ladies.

I also appreciate my fellow Brainstormers ~ Angie Arndt, Marie Coutu, and Jerusha Agen. They helped me develop various aspects of the story and description. I enjoy working with you all.

The shout-outs by the members of my Corner Room launch team got this book off to a great start. Thank you for your support.

In editing the novella, Dori Harrell of Breakout Editing corrected my atrocious grammar so *Unwrapping Hope* could be a book I'm proud to present to you.

And to all the Facebook voters who chose their favorite title when I scrambled to change it at the last minute: Thank you for *Unwrapping Hope*.

About the Author

As an author of heartwarming and award-winning historical romance, Sandra Ardoin engages readers with page-turning stories of love and faith. Rarely out of reach of a book, she's also an armchair sports enthusiast, country music listener, and seldom says no to eating out.

Visit her at www.sandraardoin.com. Sign up for the Love and Faith in Fiction Newsletter at eepurl.com/Xjqwr. Connect with Sandra on BookBub, Facebook, Twitter, and Goodreads.

Read the Beginning of A Love Most Worthy

Feminine laughter drifted across the water toward the Alaskan beach at Nome. With the faint sound, cold fingers of dread tiptoed up Rance Preston's back.

"Is that our new aunt laughing, Uncle Rance?"

Only if God had frowned on him.

Yet, he feared the buoyant sound floating over the waves of the Bering Sea did indeed come from the stranger he would marry this afternoon, a woman his friend in Seattle, Frank Connors, had assured him met his requirements for a bride.

Rance clamped a gentle hand on the cap covering the six-year-old's head. "We'll find out soon, Robbie."

He listened in vain to hear her words over the crowd scattered among dozens of miners' tents and mountains of freight—sacks and crates and machinery—sitting mere yards from the water.

The warmer temperatures had broken up the winter ice, and now steamships arrived in droves in this summer of 1900, forced to anchor farther out to sea due to Nome District's shallow harbor. Those aboard rode to the shore in lighters, the boats' flat-bottomed hulls filled with men and women intent on striking it rich in the gold rush...and one mail-order bride intent on marrying a man she had never met.

As the crew in the lead boat rowed closer, the laughing lady entertained an audience of enraptured passengers with sweeping gestures. Maybe he was wrong. Maybe she wasn't the woman he expected. Maybe, in sending for a wife, he hadn't created another nightmare for himself and the boys.

With the lighter a few yards from the beach, Rance pulled out the photograph he'd received. Strange that it showed two females, not one. When the woman in the boat looked up, he compared her face with the images and swallowed the urge to groan.

Miss Russell had arrived.

Once the lighter reached the shallowest point, men scrambled over the side. One smiling gent turned his back to Miss Russell and urged her to climb aboard. Rance stiffened. The man proposed to tote her piggyback? She shook her head, looking both embarrassed and uncertain.

It wasn't unusual to carry a woman to shore to avoid the necessity of her wading the last few feet, however, Miss Russell was Rance's responsibility now. He should be the one to bring her ashore.

The man from the boat turned and said something to her. She shrugged and allowed him to lift her from the lighter and carry her in his arms. Once they reached shore—within feet of Rance—she quickly slid from his hold and onto the beach of dark sand and small rocks. The hem of her green skirt dripped with seawater. It appeared the man's precaution had proved unsuccessful.

His future bride smiled and said, "Thank you, Mr. Digby. That was...quite an experience."

The gentleman, who was dressed more like a gambler than a miner, held out her case. "It was my pleasure to assist you, Miss Russell. I hope we'll meet again while I'm here."

Rance's breath caught as he waited for her to reject the idea of associating with another man.

She reached for the valise. "I'll be busy with my new family, sir, but I wish you a lovely stay in Nome."

Once Digby tipped his hat and walked away, Rance exhaled.

Miss Russell caught her bottom lip between her teeth. Her timidity created in him a surprising urge, a protective urge. Though his mind shouted for him to act, to reassure her, his muscles froze.

The top of the woman's head only reached his shoulder. Strands of light orange hair poked from under her hat, freed by the sea breeze. Wisps of curls, the shade of a winter sunset, blew across a face dappled with freckles. Not as winsome as the second woman in the photograph, her ordinary features helped to ease his anxiety. After all, he sought greater virtues from a wife than beauty.

At the pain of a sharp elbow from someone in the jostling crowd, he stepped forward, dragging Robbie and Davie with him. "Miss Russell?"

"Mr. Preston?" She glanced down, seeing the boys. Her expression lightened.

"Yes, ma'am. Welcome to Nome."

"Thank you." She smiled and leaned forward as if intending to hug him. When he drew back, so did she, and the smile faltered. Marriage was one thing. Affection another.

Still, those full, moon-shaped eyes, the clear blue of an afternoon sky, reeled him in like a salmon fighting the line. How could they sparkle with excitement, cast a shadow of apprehension, and glow with the warmth of a Georgia summer sun all in a matter of seconds?

"Ow. That hurts." Davie tried to pull his hand from Rance's.

"I'm sorry, Nugget." Freed from Miss Russell's gaze, he loosened his grip on the four-year-old but refused to let go. After a couple of panic-inducing experiences, he'd learned the hard way that Davie must be watched constantly or he wandered off.

Dark hair curled upward and over the bottom of Davie's cap. Rance should have given the children a haircut before Miss Russell arrived. Caring for two small boys was difficult while operating a busy store, but shaggy hair didn't make for a good impression of his parenting skills.

Setting her case on the sand beside her, she crouched to the boys' level, addressing them in turn. "You're Robbie, and you're Davie. Am I right?"

Davie broke away and wound his short arms around her neck. She gasped, then closed her eyes and returned the hug as if he were her own.

Rance's chest ached. Late night tears and drawings of family had revealed how much the boys missed the love and attention of their parents, but he hadn't fully realized their eagerness for the arrival of his bride. Having caused their loss, he would do anything to provide them with maternal affection, including marrying a woman he didn't love.

Miss Russell released Davie and rose. The scent of lilacs rose with her. Lilacs in a gold mining district. He caught himself before a snort escaped.

She approached Robbie as if intending to embrace him, too, but the older boy inched closer to Rance's side. At the boy's move, much like his own, her cheeks gave color to her otherwise pale complexion. Clasping her hands together, she looked around. "This is a bustling place."

"Increasingly so. You might want to change from that damp suit before we see the preacher."

Those big eyes grew bigger. "We're to marry today?"

"I would prefer my intended not stay alone in one of the hotels." Rance cocked his head. "Marrying me *is* why you came, isn't it?"

At the purse of her lips, that spine-crawling dread returned. He'd been duped once by a female, and his nephews had paid the price. He couldn't afford to be deceived again.

A Love Most Worthy is available on Amazon, along with Sandra's other books:
amazon.com/Sandra-Ardoin/e/B005CWP5JW